COMMITMENT

A NOVEL BY

DENNIS WECHTER

COPYRIGHT

ACKNOWLEDGEMENT

First of all, I would like to thank all those who believed in my ability as an author to write a novel. This is my first novel, and the support of others made the decision to write an easy one. I thank those who agreed to review my work in progress and offer critical thoughts. Your input was welcomed and made a difference in the final product. As always, I thank God for giving me the strength and knowledge to write from the heart. The writing process is a lonely process, and I thank those who were willing to listen to my rantings when I needed a sounding board, and not a critique. Finally, I wish to thank anyone who will read this work and share in what I consider to be an act of kindness. I wish never to take any possible audience for granted, but to always remember the who I write for, and why I write. You all occupy a special place in my heart.

Dr. Dennis Wechter

DEDICATION

This book is dedicated to all those who serve to help others achieve peace and harmony in their lives. Psychiatrists, psychologists, and mental health professionals perform an invaluable service. Their ability to understand the human condition and to have a positive impact on a person's thoughts, perceptions, feelings, and behaviors is a true gift that few possess and most give away willingly. Thank you for your service to mankind.

INTRODUCTION

His name was Chase Roman and, among other things, his life was a formidable story replete with tragedy, heartache, and complications. One might say that his circumstances were certainly more than one man should ever go through, and yet, he did with amazing grace and fortitude. Not that it didn't take a toll on him. It did, and in crushing ways. There might be some who would say that his life was no better or worse than any other person. I know better than that. I am Dr. James Styles and have been for some time his therapist. And although he might not approve of my intentions, I still feel compelled to tell his story. Don't worry, I will change the names of all the guilty parties and remain truthful to the events. I ask that you don't assume that what I will describe presents a one-sided story. It does not, for I have taken great strides to investigate all sides. So that what I represent is a balanced story. Even though I am telling it through the eyes of the Chase Roman I have come to know and respect. Chase came to me rather late in life, after his circumstances had already taken their toll on his psyche. He stayed with me for over two years. During that time, I came to know and understand how complex an individual can be and that, as he put it,sometime dreams don't come true no matter what we do. So, let's begin this journey together and discover a most enigmatic human being.

TABLE OF CONTENTS

CHAPTER ONE
THEY DON'T MAKE THEM LIKE THEY USED TO

I was having lunch with an old friend and colleague the other day who was a professor of psychology at a nearby university. He mentioned that he had a student who had approached him about her father and how she was concerned to the point of being almost afraid that he might be in serious emotional trouble. She asked if he could help. He told her he did not think it would be appropriate for him to get involved with her father. Then he told her he had a friend who was a therapist and he might be willing to talk with her father.

I reminded my colleague that I was winding down my practice and not accepting any new clients. That after twenty years of practice, I was about ready to retire. But, I said, as a favor to you, I will speak with this gentleman. My friend said thank you and he would let his student know and give her my contact information. I said that would be fine. In a few days, my secretary let me know that I had a new client coming in on Monday. His name was Chase Roman.

"Chase." I said, " can you tell me what brings you here today?" "Honestly," he said, I'm not sure." "Well, do you know what we do here for our patients?"

"I can only imagine, but I'm more that convinced that it can't be good for me." I told Chase that I thought that was an unfair characterization, and that we genuinely care about each and every one of our patients.

"I'm sorry Doc, I didn't mean to offend." "Please tell me, just what is it that you do here?" "Well," I said, "We try to help our patients overcome negative situations in their lives. As a licensed therapist, It is my job to create a safe environment for my patients in every session. I do this so that my patients feel comfortable sharing anything and everything that they are struggling with in their lives. I believe that through qualified discussions, over time, patients can be healed or made whole and may return to society as productive citizens." "Wow," said Chase, "that's a lot of responsibility." I said, "yes it is, and I take my work very seriously." "I can appreciate your position, Doc." "You don't mind if I call you Doc do you?" "Not at all," I said. "If you don't mind me calling you Chase." "That's my name Doc." "Ok then, now that you have had the opportunity to know about me, Don't you think it would be fair, if I could find out a little more about you." "What would you like to know?" "For starters, how is it that you find yourself here today?" "Doc, I am here at the behest of my children." "What do your children want you to do?" I asked, "My children are concerned that I am manically depressed and have been for some time." "Do you think that it's true what you children are saying about you?" Chase said, "I don't really know, I'm trying to be the good guy here, but, for the life of me, I don't know why they think I'm depressed." "Well, I would assume that they have seen a number of signs and perhaps activities for which they think might qualify you for some professional help." "Well," Chase said, "How did they find you, and what makes you think you can help me." "The how, is not important," I said, "And, just for the record, I am a pretty successful therapist, with over twenty years of experience in the field." "I am confident that I can help you, However, I can't tell you definitively until we have more serious conversations." "Doc," Chase said, "I think that is a very fair position from which to start our relationship together." I said, "terrific."

Chased asked me when I thought we should start, I told him, "let's have a cup of tea and discuss it further." "Tea," he said, "Doc, don't you have anything a little stronger that tea." "I'm afraid not," I said, "but, I make a pretty strong cup of tea." Chase said, "I'm sure you do, I'll have the tea." And with that, our relationship began.

Chase Roman was born in New York City in the 1950s. His family was of European descent, strong, hard-working people with absolutely no imagination.

His mother gave birth to him by walking ten blocks to the hospital once her contractions began. She didn't have a driver's license, and taking a cab didn't seem like the thing to do.

On her journey to the hospital, she almost gave birth around block number six and as she fell to the ground in great pain, a couple of Samaritan citizens came to her rescue. They brought her to the hospital just in time for Chase to be born. Where was his father… away on business?

He often left his wife to go on these junkets as they were, without nary a word to the family. I guess his mother had gotten used to her situation, as she rarely spoke about it to her parents or her children. Chase would recall in one of our sessions that she always seemed to be a little afraid of her husband, and as a result, he did pretty much anything he wanted to do. My impression of her was as a woman who found herself needing to manage both sides of parenthood. She was, after all, a woman of "great stock," as she called it. I only knew her through the reference that Chase made after he started seeing me for therapy. I guess, in some sense, he always wanted her to understand what he was going through. According to him, in his family, they never acknowledged or discussed emotional disorders.

I know from his sessions with me he came from a most dysfunctional family. However, he rarely blamed them for his experiences as a child. Quite the contrary, he erroneously believed that he had a perfectly normal childhood. Even after a short time with him, I knew better.

Truth be told, he was afraid of his father and regarded his mother as a weak individual who was always trying to please everybody, without regard to her own needs.

Chase changed schools several times in the city, with no explanation. He also moved several times in the city and when he asked his mother why one day after the sixth or seventh move, she just replied," that's what your father wants" It was never about what anybody else wanted.

Because of this unusual thing his father had, Chase never really could develop any friendships. He would go to school, come home, and just be in his room. This was his normal process, and as such, he developed some rather bad eating habits. His family only occasionally sat down for a family dinner. When they did, there was never much conversation. Certainly not the "Madison Avenue" advertising model of the family dynamic. His family dynamic was certainly not "Father Knows Best" (*TV show from the 1950s*), it was more like father doesn't care! Chase once told me that he was convinced his father would prefer to be anywhere else in the world rather than with his family. Most of the time he was silent in the home, only talking when it was absolutely necessary. "Did your relationship with your father ever reach a caustic level?" "It might have," Chase said, "but I was too young, or too scared to do anything about it." "I guess the whole family was, so we let him just be what he was going to be, and never questioned his decisions." "Chase, I think I can help you, if you will let me." "But you must understand that this will take time," "How much time?" Chase asked. "I honestly can't say," "But I promise you, it will be worth your time and effort." Chase smiled and said, "Doc, I'm all yours." I was thinking to myself, what might I have gotten myself into." Only time would tell.

Part of my discussion with Chase centered on the idea that he held his mother partly responsible for a couple of conditions he went through as a child. Even though he told me he loved her, and she said often that she loved him.

He even related a story to me about a time when he was in the car with his mother. She finally got her driver's license because his father was not around enough when she needed to go someplace, and she was tired of taking the bus or a cab. So they were in the car and he noticed that his mother was no longer smoking. She was a two-pack-a-day smoker, and the anti-smoking campaigns had just begun. Surprise filled him as he noticed his mother was no longer smoking. When he asked her why she stopped smoking, she told him that at her last medical checkup; the doctor told her that if she didn't stop smoking, some other woman would raise her children. She left the doctor's office and never lit up a cigarette again. She did not say it outright, but we knew she did it because she loved us.

By the way, the "Us" relates to Chase's brother, Michael. He was a year older than Chase and seemed pretty normal. At lease that is what Chase had to say about him. Chase had little more to say about him. That to me was strange. Since not having any outside friends, one would think that Chase would be much closer to his brother. I wanted to pursue that topic during one of our sessions, but Chase said, "let sleeping dogs lie." I don't quite know what he meant by that statement, but I assumed there were issues between them that Chase just did not want to talk about. I would come to learn that there were several issues that Chase did not want to talk about. However, there were some issues that he was willing to talk about. One of the earliest issues that Chase was willing to talk about was his relationship with his father.

He told me from the very beginning of that conversation that his father thought little of him. I said, "is it possible that you are just projecting your feelings about your father, while not really understanding the man?"

He responded, "look Doc, how would you feel about a person who was always cold, non-nurturing, always distant, never available, and once said to my mother that he did not want a second child."

I said, "I don't know enough about the man to render any kind of opinion. And, since you rarely want to talk about him, I will wait until you have more to say about him." He never talked much more about his father unless he absolutely needed to make a point. The one point he did make was that he knew his father was a "bag man" for the mob. He never mentioned how he found out, or how that affected his relationship with his father. He said that he was afraid of him and usually kept his distance when his father was home. During this conversation, he also told me that never once did he ever call his father "Dad," "Daddy," or even "Father" From his earliest recollection, he called him, by his first name Joseph.

CHAPTER TWO
WHAT'S WRONG WITH ME

I wanted to discuss Chase's father in much greater depth, but he told me that maybe a little later. I knew he had more to say about his father, but I chose not to push the issue. He needed to move back to his mother. I knew he had great affection for her, but he chose to not relate that regularly. Still, I knew he cared about her position in the family. Remembering that she was much the matriarch of the family, out of necessity, rather than desire. Her father had left her mother many years before Chase was born. Never saying a word of goodbye, but just not coming home one day.

Chase knew she had a great hatred for her father, and rarely mentioned his name, even when Chase would go with her to visit her mother, his grandmother. Her mother never remarried, since her husband never sought a divorce. He just left and started a new life in another country. He found this out because Chase's aunt found him after years of searching for him. My grandmother died basically alone and poor. Chase told me that his father never cared about what happened to his mother-in-law, and he knew that his mother always held that against him. He also told me he told her to never mention her again in his presence. His mother just took it and moved on. This, Chase said, was her usual method of dealing with uneasy circumstances. In some sense, Chase said that he could never understand why his mother never left his father, but in those days, divorce was not something that was easily gained. He also felt that since she was afraid of him, she might have been afraid of what he might have done if she sought a divorce. He told me that in some sense; he held her weakness against her for not being able to establish a cohesive family environment. But she did what she could. He believed that his home life was just a constant tension convention, and probably led to the next thing he wanted to reveal to me.

He told me that as a child he suffered from excessive bed- wetting. This became a constant issue for his father who would often say, "what's wrong with this child" His mother did not have a satisfactory answer until sometime later when the doctor told her that Chase had an underdeveloped bladder, and that it would take time for this situation to end, but that it would end. Meanwhile, the hurtful comments from his father made it difficult for his mother to cope with this sensitive condition, even breaking down and crying. Chase said he hated his father for his lack of understanding and sympathy. This was the first time I saw tears come from Chase, but it would not be the last time.

After a couple of years beyond when children normally stop wetting the bed, Chase's issue resolved itself. But he never forgave his father for the way he made him and his mother feel.

This issue was an important first step for me in trying to break through the defensive veneer that Chase always had employed. I knew he wanted to talk about the more pervasive issue in his life, and I was prepared to open that chapter.

Chase told me he never felt that he had any outlet for his anger and frustration, so he stayed in his room and consumed more food than he should have, causing his weight to increase dramatically. He reached a point where he simply could not stop. I was very interested in how this affected his emotional state, since, when I first saw him, he was an adult of what would be a normal weight. I asked him how bad did it get, and he told me he used food for comfort every time he had to spend time in his house. Every time his father would say something mean or cruel, which was becoming the norm now. And every time his mother would not defend his behavior. Again, the "what is wrong with this child!" became the daily mantra.

Chase said he felt trapped and would never have happiness in his life. I told him I had great empathy for his childhood situation, and that I was sorry that more professionals were not available at the time to help him. He told me he could not remember a happy moment in the first ten years of his life. According to him, he dealt with his situation by utilizing humor as a defense mechanism. He also told me that since he changed schools so often, he would have to endure a considerable "fat slurs and jokes" before he could use humor to make his classmates stop. This did not, however, end the sessions of crying he went through when he got home each day. I reminded him of how cruel kids can be and that they loved to focus on other people's weaknesses in order to pump themselves up.

He told me he understood that, but it was little consolation. He also told me he rarely spoke to his parents about this situation, choosing instead to suffer in silence. I knew we had a lot of work to do.

CHAPTER THREE
A BREAK IN THE ACTION

About six months into his therapy, I asked him, "when did you gain some genuine sense of who you were, and what your possibilities might be?"

He responded with the following story. "When I was eleven years old, my parents sent me away to summer sleep-away camp." I asked, "how did you feel about that?" He said that he had never been to a summer camp, let alone a "sleep-away" camp, and he just figured they wanted to get rid of him for six weeks. However, he found the camp rather boring and trying because there were some camp events he could not take part in because of his weight. So, he usually talked his way out of them, preferring to return to his cabin to read.

I said, "didn't this make you even more separated from others you might have made friends with?" He replied, "to be honest, I could have cared less about my fellow campers, as I felt I had nothing in common with them." I said, "perhaps you might have missed the possibility of forming a genuine friendship." "Well," he said, "I formed a friendship with one particular camper named Skylar." I said, "Why did you feel the need to form this friendship?" "Because he had a guitar with him, and he knew how to play it!" "This interested you?" "Are you kidding! It was the sixties and guitars were all the rage!." I asked, "so what did you do about it?." "I begged him to teach me how to play." He told me "Only if you are serious about it."

He said that he convinced Skylar to teach him and that he would be a serious student. Skylar agreed, and as Chase related, "this changed my life forever."

When Chase got home, he begged his parents to buy him a guitar. He promised them he would study every day and learn to play the instrument very well.

He told me his dad said that would not happen because he didn't want to hear the noise around the house. Chase said, "why do you care, since you are never home?" That did not go over well with his father. However, his mother took him aside later and said to him, "I don't want you to worry. I will find a way to get you that guitar." I said, "how did that make you feel when she told you that?" He said he could hardly believe that she would go against his father when he decided something.

But he believed she saw the sincerity in his eyes and speech, so she went to bat for him. He noted it was one of the few times that he was proud of his mother. However, Chase noted she paid a price for that decision as yet another argument that he could plainly hear. They had lots of arguments, sometimes screaming and throwing things. Chase said he would just stay in his room until it was over. Sometimes that shouting was too much for him and he would break down and cry. Eventually, he told me he became sort of numb to the arguments as they were so frequent.

I told him he had developed a coping mechanism for the pain. "Yeah" he said. "I guess I had a lot of coping mechanisms." I knew how he meant that, but I could see the pain in his eyes when he referenced the events. As the argument over the guitar issue became more heated, Chase wanted to go out into the living room and stop it. But the actual chance he might get a guitar stopped him from doing just that. Once again, he related to me how much he hated his father. Finally, after some yelling by both his parents, his father gave in and said, "he'd better learn how to play that thing and not just cost me money for no reason." He told me that his mother assured her husband he was serious, and that she believed he could actually learn to play the instrument.

Chase said, "they did not know how serious I was." Finally the day came for Chase and his mother to go to the guitar store. But it was not a music store, but a pawn shop. Chase said that his mother told him they could get a better deal there than in a music store. Honestly, he didn't care about the guitar's origin as long as he got one that day. He got one that day. He mentioned it was a guitar that was inexpensive, but it played well and allowed him to purchase a small guitar amplifier because of its affordable cost. "According to him, he was in ecstatic "I felt like I was in heaven! Nothing else in my life mattered. Every morning, before school, I would put it on for an hour."

He said it was not long before he had totally burned through the study guides his friend Skylar had given him and was searching for more materials. As he gained more materials and skills, he said he would listen to the radio and learn every song he could. He said he developed quite a talent for listening to a song and intuitively knowing how to play it. "After a while, I could play dozens of popular rock songs and ballads" "It was then, I decided to become a rock star!" "OK, I said, and how has that worked out for you?" He said,. "well you know the dreams of a child don't always work out the way they were planned. But he said, "The guitar has been with me basically my whole life and I will die with it." So I said, "no regrets?" He said, "not for a minute. You see, the guitar and my music have been the only constant in my life. It is my one true anchor, and when everyone else has let me down or abused me, I have always known that my music and guitar could never do that." I said I understood and left it at that. I now know how Chase has survived his circumstances.

CHAPTER FOUR
SOMETIMES LIFE IS NOT FAIR

As much as I was happy to see some joy enter Chase's life, I knew there would be more issues to deal with. "As you know and agreed to, I have interviewed your family, and they think you are seriously depressed." "To be honest, there is one more issue I would like to discuss with you." "Only one more," I remarked. "Well, one more related to my adolescent period." "I am ready and willing to listen to anything you wish to discuss."

"I will tell you something now that I have told no one else, ever!" I said, "This sounds like a critical issue for you. May I ask why you have felt the need to never talk about it with anyone else?"

"Because" he said, "it has been to heinous an act for me to talk about, but I know I must tell the story and I hope you are receptive to what I have to say." I said, "I will always have your best interests at heart and everything we speak about will always be in total confidence. He said, "fair enough" As he told this story, I couldn't help but notice the tears that were welling up in his eyes. I leaned over and handed him a box of tissues, as I have been down this road before with other patients. He began this way, "when I was twelve years old, I was attending a private school as my brother and I had always done.

The school was In the city and several blocks from our home. I usually took a cab, or sometimes rode the bus, but this day, it was so beautiful that I decided to walk home. My brother always had stuff to do with his friends and never wanted me to accompany him. It was ok; I was used to being alone. Spring was just beginning and some days the city was incredibly beautiful. It was also a different time, when people could walk around the city and, mostly, feel safe."

"As I was turning a corner and walking by some "brownstones" as they were called. Basically, city row houses with apartments above the street and usually one below street level. A person came up behind me and forced me down into one of the lower apartment areas.

He said, "Don't say a word, or I will hurt you." I was so scared; I didn't believe I could speak even if I wanted to." By this time, Chase was crying, and I asked if this was too much for him to go on. He paused briefly and said he could continue. "the person then pulled my pants and underwear down and as I am aware now, he raped me. He sodomized me, and when he was through, he just walked away. I could not move for several moments while my brain was trying to process what had just happened." I said how sorry I was that he had to go through that event, and I asked why he didn't immediately seek help from law enforcement.

He told me he felt too embarrassed to talk about it to anyone. I said, "so you have kept this incident hidden in you psyche all these years, and have never told a soul about it," He said, "I could barely understand what had happened to me, and for years, I blamed myself for walking home that day." I told him I understood and assured that his response was not in the least unusual and that many rape victims never come forward. I decided we needed a break. I sat as he continued to cry until he had expressed all his emotions. As we returned to the session, I asked Chase if there was anything else about his adolescence he wished to discuss. Chase told me he had one more story to tell. I said let's table this until next week. As he left, I was full of emotion myself. I thought how could so many negative events occur to one person. I needed to take a break from all this negative energy myself. But I knew that after today's session, Chase and I would be linked together for a very long time.

As our next session began, I told Chase that I thought he was a very brave soul, and I felt honored that he would share these intimate secrets with me. He said, "Doc, I now believe that you will always be in my corner no matter what I tell you." "For that, and perhaps more than for any other reason, you have my eternal gratitude." I said, "OK Chase, whenever you are ready."

As he began another story, I sensed that this was going to be rough, so I tossed him the box of tissues. He nodded in acknowledgement.

He said that he was thinking over the week, should he tell this story. I asked, "What would stop you from sharing?" "Well," he said, this event surrounds itself in some aspect of religion." "And, why would that be significant, I have heard of religion." "Ok, you asked for it."

He began to tell the story of his experience as a Jewish child growing up in New York. "I remember going to Hebrew school with my brother. "We went for three days every week, in preparation for the Jewish tradition of Bar Mitzvah." "So far," I said, "the story sounds pretty normal." "I am aware of the Jewish religion and its traditions." "Ok," Chase said, "So after two years of study, the day finally came for my brother to have his Bar Mitzvah." Chase told me it was a beautiful ceremony and his brother did quite well. I said, "Mazel Tov." Chase just looked as me and laughed. It was nice seeing him laugh, he did it so infrequently. "Again," I said, "I don't see anything wrong." "Just hang in there, " he said, "I promise it will suck soon." So Chase went on to describe an incredible celebration for his brother at the Waldorf Astoria in New York City. "It was magic that night, and it was also the first time I ever sang in public." "seriously," I said. "Yep, I walked right up to the bandstand and asked the band leader if I could sing a song." "Look at you!" I said, "Being all brave and everything." "Yes, I was barely twelve years old, But I saw a chance, and I took it." "Actually, it wasn't such a big chance, I was the brother of the guest of honor, and my father was paying for everything. So…" "So, you performed." "I did." "Do you remember what song you sang that night?" "Yes," Chase said, "I sang; I Left My Heart In San Francisco, a big hit for Tony Bennet." "What a great story." I said. "So, not to sound like a broken record, but I still don't see a tragedy here." "Just hold on," Chase said, "I was developing the back story for you." "Ok, sorry."

"So it is a year later, and I am now studying for my turn in the Temple." "After all, what Jewish boy does not want to be called "A Man."

"I studied hard and I thought I was ready" "However a few weeks before my ceremony was to happen, My mother came to me and said, "I'm sorry, but we are not going to be able to have a celebration for you." I said, "What do you mean, no celebration?" My mother said, "You can go through the ceremony, but no celebration party for you." I said, "Why?" She said, "I don't know for sure; this is just what you father has told me to tell you."

"Doc, I went ballistic, screaming, running through the house, and yelling, "This is not fair!" "I went to my room, and just sat on my bed and cried." "Chase., I am so sorry you had to go through this experience." "I could not understand what I had done wrong to deserve this." "Did my parents just not love me or care for me at all." "Chase," I said, "Please don't do this to yourself, you don't need to relive this moment." "You are wrong, Doc, " "I most assuredly need to relive this moment, so I remember not to forget, how I was treated for most of my adolescent life." "May I ask you; how did you finally cope with what happened to you?" "Well," Chase said, "I never went back to that Temple. I never studied another Hebrew word; I threw away all my Hebrew books. I told my mother to send back any gifts I had received in advance of my big day." "That was a big deal, I was going to use that Bar Mitzvah cash to buy a new guitar." "And I basically gave up on the Jewish religion altogether." " I never wanted to hear another " Old Testament story again" "And, as you might imagine, I hated both of my parents so much, I didn't know how I could continue to live with them." "Chase, I'm sure your mother was very sorry for what happened to you." "Well if she was," Chase said, "She never showed it. She just went on like nothing happened." "OK, Chase, I think we need a break. Can I fix you some tea?" "Chase looked at me and calmed down a bit. "Yes," he said sheepishly, "I would like some tea," and I thought we might have to call it a day, and let things rest a bit. "Chase, can we pick this up next week?" "Sure, he said." "Are you alright?" I asked. "Yes, I'll be fine, I'm always fine." Many hours now in the book with Chase told me differently, He was far from fine. "All right," I said, "I told him that in our next session, we would move on to the next chapter in his life. As he left, I couldn't help but think how complicated a life he had led and felt a reverence for his ability to get through it all. I was excited to move into the next segment of his life.

CHAPTER FIVE
THE NEED TO MOVE ON

As I waited for Chase to arrive for his next appointment, I couldn't help but read my notes and try to make sense of what could have kept him from seeking help in the past. There was no doubt in my mind that he, if anybody, deserved to be seen by a qualified therapist. I was also quite glad that he had stayed with me and felt comfortable relating his life's story to me. I did not know what was to come, but I was eager to be involved in his story.

When Chase arrived, I greeted him cordially and offered him some tea. He said he would love some. So we shared a cup of tea and I asked him how he was doing and was he ready to continue. He said he was doing as well as could be expected and was indeed ready to move on. I expressed my gratitude to him for his willingness to share his story with me, and I assured him that nothing said in our sessions would ever be made public. He said he understood and believed what I had said was truthful. I leaned over and handed him the tissue box and he looked at it and just said thanks. "So," I said. "What would you like to talk about today? He said that he felt the need to deal with some tragedies of his high school life. I said "Go right ahead, I'm listening.

He then related to me that his high school experience was, mostly, a lost cause, and in some circumstances, a tragedy. I said I was very interested in how he reached that conclusion. Ok, he said, "By the time I entered high school, we had moved to Maryland and I would attend a high school in Washington D.C., about three blocks from the White House."

I said it sounded nice, and he said that Washington D.C. was indeed a beautiful place, but the school was another story. A prep school steeped in history.

"For God's sake," he said, The average age of the teachers was two years past death." "My chemistry teacher worked for the FBI and discovered marijuana in the early 1900s". "And to add insult to everything else, it was an all-boys school. "Ok," I said, "did you have to go there?" "Well that's what my mother and father wanted us to do." "So," I said, "There was no room for discussion." "Exactly," he said. "alright, what was so bad about the school, other than the out of touch teachers and the no girls' rule?" Chase told me that at the time, he was not interested in school. He was a confirmed "Hippie." Wow, there's a flashback. And the idea of wearing a suit every day to cover the uniform code was abhorrent to him.

Chase was, after all, part of the sixties' counterculture. I said, "Ok, so there were some issues with the school. I don't see the tragedy." He agreed that the school was not the tragedy. However, what followed contributed to his negative feelings about this institution. "Being steeped in tradition and a first class "preppy" environment," "You can imagine how they felt about "Hippies.""

"They didn't like them" I asked. "You could say that." "As a matter of fact, the jocks in the school would go to Georgetown on Friday nights to seek out and beat up Hippies." "It was a sort of sport for them, and I was playing in a confirmed counterculture hippie band that performed in Georgetown regularly."

"I never understood why the administration never forced me to cut my hair. Maybe it had something to do with the connections my father had in D.C., as he was still connected to the mob. Chase told me that even with the stress of being the only hippie in his school, and the long hair issue, it was still not a tragedy. "Ok" I said, please tell me what tragic thing happened that were related to the school. "During my junior year, while my band was playing in Georgetown, our bass player tried to score some heroin. He was a substance misuser, and it ended his life way too early. Our lead singer went with him to a different section of Georgetown, where he was sure they could score some drugs. We told them we would meet them at the White Castle, a popular spot in Georgetown because it was open all night." I said, "So far, I'm with you. I don't approve, but I understand the drug culture of the time." He then told me that every night, a bunch of jocks from his school were just in Georgetown that night looking for hippies to beat up. Our bass player and lead singer wound up scoring their drugs, and when they were walking to the White Castle, they encountered the Jocks from my school. Not wanting to waste a good beat down, they confronted his bandmates. During the ensuing fight, because his lead singer was never one to back down from a fight, one jock stabbed him and killed him! "do you understand! Students from my school killed the lead singer of my band!!! "He confided in me that upon learning about the incident, he experienced a crushing feeling, only to realize days later that it was a student from his own school."

He found out because the police came to the school and arrested the student. I said, "I have no words to express how sorry I am to hear this story. You are correct when you describe this event as a tragedy.." "I assume you went to the funeral." I said. "Yes," he said, "and my parents said they were sorry, but not much else." "After that, the band broke up. Rest In Peace–The Chosen Few." This, I knew, was a very difficult story for him to tell me. I said we should take a break, and he agreed. I swear, I do not know how Chase made it through high school. When we resumed, I asked if it was time to move on. "One more story." He said. I said, "are you sure you want to continue down this high school confidential?" He said yes because the next story was a life-changing moment. I told him whenever he was ready. He related to me that during his senior year, the guidance counselor called his parents in for a conference. During that conference, in which Chase was present, the guidance counselor said to his parents that under no circumstances were they to consider sending him to college. They said he would fail miserably. Send him to the army. Chase said, "The army, which would mean Vietnam." I thought to myself, that's what the army needed: another hippie in Vietnam. Chase, what would have happened if you were not able to graduate high school? In those days, as I have read, high school dropouts were fair game for the army. Chase told me that it was a moot point because his age group was entered into the lottery system, a system that ran for two years. I said I think I remember that event. They would come on the television and pull balls out of a cage to match birthdates. Each ball had a number that corresponded to a day of the year. "That's correct." Chase said. So, I asked what happened. Chase told me that as each ball was pulled, none of them were matching his birthday….that is until they pulled the last ball. "You mean you pulled number 365?" "That's correct." "Wow!" I said. "You certainly were the lucky one. Chase told me that with that event behind him, he could concentrate on his future.

"Also, for the first time in my crazy life," Chase said, "I heard my mother read this guidance counselor the riot act and said things in my defense I never thought she would say."

He told me that on the way home, she told him not to listen to that person and that he could be anything he wanted to be as long as he worked hard to achieve the goal. "That day," Chase said, "I developed a new appreciation for my mother." I Asked if there was anything else he wanted to cover about this period in his life, and he told me that after a brief break, he would be ready to move on. I agreed and said that I could use a break as well. During the break, my mind was racing with the events that were just presented. I wondered what future events could befall this unique individual. I didn't have to wait very long.

CHAPTER SIX

THE LOST YEAR

This morning, when Chase arrived, I greeted him in our usual manner. We had a cup of tea and then he asked me a question. "Doctor, he seemed quite formal, can I discuss anything with you?" I said, "Chase, we have been down a very long road and I believe that we now have a significant history together." "Wouldn't you agree?" He said, "of course I agree. But this may be beyond even your level of comprehension." I said, "Why don't you tell me, and I will do my professional best to understand." He agreed and began describing a nightmare he was having. I asked him how long he had been having this nightmare. He told me for just a few weeks. He thought it would go away, but it keeps re-appearing. I convinced him to tell me about it the best way he could. "Well," he said, "it always starts the same, with a boy running down a street or long driveway screaming don't go!!!"

I asked him what happens next? "He reaches the end of the road and falls to his knees and just sobs uncontrollably. Then I wake up."

"Is there more?" I asked. "No," he said, "there is never anymore. What do you think this means?" I told him there could be several varied reasons he was having the dream, but it has importance to him, and therefore it might be worth pursuing. Then I ventured into an area that was outside my wheelhouse. "Chase, have you ever heard the term Dissociative Amnesia?" He said no, but if it related to him, he wanted more information. I told him that with everything he had been through, I believe he has blocked some memories that are too hard to deal with.

He told me he didn't think that was possible. I said yes it is, and as a matter of fact, Dissociative Amnesia is a real symptom and not as rare as one would imagine. "Well, how do you deal with it?" he asked. I told him I had a colleague who was a psychiatrist at the university. If he felt ok with it, I could call him and see if he would be interested in seeing you. Chase agreed, so I made plans to contact my colleague, Dr. Mike Stanford.

A week later, Dr. Stanford agreed to see Chase and said he wouldn't mind if I attended the session as well. I told him I would contact Chase and set up the appointment for the following week. As I hung up the phone, I considered my actions and motives. Was this going to be a good thing for Chase, or could it open up wounds that might never heal? Finally, I knew that as a therapist, my responsibility was to help Chase become as whole a person as he could be. I set up the appointment with Dr. Stanford, and with Chase. I truly did not know what the outcome would be, but deep inside, I was excited about the process.

Another week went by, and the day of the procedure finally arrived. I met Chase at Dr. Stanford's office on the grounds of the university. I said, "thank you for agreeing to do this. Are you nervous? "He said, "no, but I am curious." "How do you know this will work?" I said, "there are no guarantees for a procedure such as this." "We just engage the process and see where it leads us." "Does that sound good to you?" He said, "Let's get this started."

As we entered Dr. Stanford's office, he was sitting at his desk looking over some notes I had sent him. He rose to meet us and warmly greeted Chase. Chase smiled and said it was a pleasure. He led us over to a sitting area with a long, very comfortable-looking couch and two comfortable chairs. He asked if this setting was acceptable. We both nodded, and we sat down. Chase intuitively knew he was to sit on the couch. Dr. Stanford began, "Chase, thank you for coming in today. We know it was a decision that required a great deal of thought. We want you to be completely at ease with what is about to happen. I rarely have observers during this process but considering the relationship you have developed with Dr. Styles, I thought he would aid in your comfort." Chase said thank you and he was glad to have me in the room. Dr. Stanford asked if he was ready and Chase said yes. "Fine, then we shall proceed." I want you to understand the clinical aspect of regression hypnosis."

"You mean you will not ask me to cluck like a chicken whenever I hear a phone ring?" "No" said Dr. Stanford. "We in the psychiatric community take this process seriously. We have used it successfully many times, and we firmly believe in the efficacy of its results." Chase said, "I'm glad to hear that, and I was only kidding about the chicken routine. Please proceed." Dr. Stanford got up and closed some very heavy curtains and the room became very dark. He turned on a very soothing amber light near the couch and asked Chase to lie down. He then asked Chase to close his eyes and try to be silent. "Chase, I want you to listen to the sound of my voice and relax your whole body. All you can hear is the sound of my voice, allowing you to block out any other sounds or noise. In the next few minutes, you will lose control over your body. You will no longer feel any body parts and you won't be able to move them because they are not here. Actually, I was beginning to lose the feeling in my body as I totally relaxed. I could certainly see how this process could make a person compliant with suggestions. After a few minutes, when Dr. Stanford was sure Chase was in a quasi-trance state, he was ready to take him to the dream in question. "Chase," he said. "I want you to remember the dream about the boy in the driveway. Can you see him?" Chase, after a minute or so said, "Yes I can. He is standing behind a car and screaming." "What is he screaming Chase?" "He is screaming at the person in the car not to leave." "Chase, can you see who is in the car?" After a few seconds, Chase screamed, "Yes!, Oh my God, it's my mother! And she is driving away!" The screaming continued, "Why are you leaving me? Why would she leave me? Where is she going? He cried actual tears. "I don't understand, what is happening!" "Chase, what is happening now?" asked Dr. Stanford. "She is driving away! No, no, no come back! Please come back!" "Chase, what are you doing now" he asked. "I am running after her, down the back driveway, past the neighbors' houses." "Wait!, please wait for me!" Chase then related that she turned down the street and sped away. When he got to the end of the back driveway, he fell to his knees and cried unconsolably.

At this point, he stopped screaming and was just crying. "Chase," Dr. Stanford said, "I want you to calm down slowly and leave the scene you have just been describing." I want you to come back to this room and this couch. Slowly, that's it. Just listen to the sound of my voice and return to us." After a few minutes, Chase calmed down and opened his eyes. Still tearful, he said, "I didn't remember that happening. Why Dr. Stanford couldn't I remember that event?" Dr. Stanford told him that the experience was just too painful and his mind blocked the incident altogether until he could cope with the aftermath. Chase told us he remembered going to sleep in his aunt's house and the next morning she told him that his mother had to go away for a while, but she would come back for him and his brother soon.

"Do you know when? 'Chase asked. "I'm not sure of the exact time," his aunt responded, "but you know she loves you and your brother, and I will ensure that you are well taken care of in my house until she returns."

After a while, Chase sat up and had some water. I asked if he was alright, and he said not really, but he would be. I assured him that indeed he would be all right soon. We left Dr. Stanford's office after thanking him for his compassion. He told Chase that he wished him only the best, and he was available any time he needed to talk. I also thanked my friend and colleague and said we would speak soon. Outside the building I was almost afraid to let Chase go. He seemed so fragile. I asked. "Are you going to be alright?" "I could stay with you for a while if you need me to." He assured me he would be all right and he would see me at our next meeting. As I watched him walk away, I couldn't help feeling that somehow I had done some damage to him. He looked so lost. I hoped with all my heart that he wouldn't hate me for bringing him to a process that created such pain. I will find out in our next meeting.

CHAPTER SEVEN
THE NEXT PHASE

We were never to speak about the events that transpired in Dr. Stanford's office. I just assumed that Chase had filed it away in whatever compartment he created in his mind. He wanted to move on to what he called the next phase in his life. As we shared a cup of tea, he shared…

"I considered this next phase of my life critically important because I knew I would be solely responsible for making all the decisions."

He told me that after finishing high school, he decided to attend college in Florida. His parents had already left Washington D.C. for Atlanta, Boston, and eventually Florida. "I must add that I did not know they were going to move to Florida," Chase said. "They were in Boston and Atlanta on business. They left a year earlier, choosing to leave the house for my brother and I as we finished school.

I did not know my brother's plans, but I was off to college in Florida" He then told me that after a year of attending college in Dade County Florida (basically Miami), his parents convinced him to move up to Broward County, switch colleges, and move in with them. He agreed on the condition that he could come and go as he pleased. They agreed, so he spent year two in Broward County, Florida.

Chase took the time to remind me he was still playing guitar and had never lost his desire to be a "rock star." "I did not know, he said, that my time would come sooner than I expected." I said, "please elaborate." He told me the manager of a show group that needed a guitar player had contacted him. They were to play in the Miami area for a few months in order to get the shows perfect. Then, they had scheduled to start an extensive road trip.

"I couldn't believe what I was hearing," he said. "The chance to play in a show band and tour the country! I jumped at the chance to audition for this show." He told me he knew his long years of studying and playing would pay off someday. At the audition, the musical director, who was the keyboard player, handed him a book of musical charts and gave him a few minutes to get settled. Then, he said, "Alright, show number one." Everybody ready? Count it off, please." He said, "we were off. I couldn't believe how good these charts were." "Very clean and accurate." I said, "So you were happy?"

"Happy doesn't do it justice. I was playing a professional show in a band, complete with a horn section." "I was a sucker for a horn section, as my true love was R & B horn bands." "I got through the first show with almost no errors." I said, "That must have made you feel proud that you hard work was finally paying off." He agreed, and the manager told the band to take a break after the first show. "As I went out of the rehearsal hall, the other musicians in the band complemented me on my Skillset." "I felt so at home playing these songs, and I really wanted this show."

He paused, and I said, "So, what happened? After a few minutes, the manager came out and expressed their impression of his performance. They offered me the position. "I was ecstatic as I accepted the position." They were pleased and told him that a rehearsal schedule would begin soon and their first job in Miami was in four weeks. Meanwhile, they had to be fitted to show costumes and pictures. I said, "congratulations on your decision to follow your heart." "Oh, did I mention that by this time in my life I had lost a ton of weight and was excited about new show clothes? I said, "it looks like your dreams were finally becoming a reality." He said, "I guess so. Especially about the part where I told my parents that I was leaving college and going on the road." "How did they respond?" I asked. "Well," he said, "You would think they would be happy for me I had finally found a dream I could pursue."

"I take it by your attitude. They weren't receptive to your plan." "Oh no," he said. "They did everything they could to talk me out of going." He told me they said that leaving college was the worst thing he could do, and this would not last, and then what was he going to do? I could sense a whole new level of frustration was developing, and it would not end well. I could not have been more correct. Chase told me that after an extended period of back and forth arguing, he finally told them to stop. He had decided, and he was going.

The next day, Chase planned to move in with a friend for the time he would be in Miami. "When I left," he said, "I did not speak to my parents for almost a year. I had never felt more alone than during that brief period before I left for the road." "I never even called them or my brother the day I left" "Great! send off, right!" I said I was sorry that his parents were not more supportive. He said it was par for the course. Our session time was about over and I told Chase that I looked forward to hearing about his road experiences during our next session.

CHAPTER EIGHT

THE ROAD

When Chase showed up for his session today, he seemed unusually happy. Instinctively, I knew why. Chase had told me some time ago that the one true love in his life was his music. So, it was logical for me to assume that he had been thinking about his life in music. I was excited to hear what he had to say, especially since the recent events with Dr. Stanford. I hoped we could get through a complete session with no drama. He deserved it, and I was looking forward to what he had to say.

He came in and we shared a cup of tea. Then I said, "Chase, I am so glad to see you today and in what appears to be a festive mood." He replied, "Thanks Doc, I am in a pretty good mood and looking forward to our session today." I said, "then let's begin" "First, during our last session, you had determined that you could no longer live with you parents." "Can you tell me how that made you feel."

Chase took a minute and then replied, "At first, I was angry that they could not understand what was important to me. They once again wanted to control me and my destiny." "I can see how that might make you angry," I said. He continued, "they wanted to maintain control of what was best for me based upon their standards. They never realized or accepted that I could be in control of my life and accept the responsibilities that went along with my choices." "I knew I would no longer accept their decisions, and therefore, I had to leave." "I need to add," he said. "That I never regretted that decision for a single minute."

I asked him how he resolved that decision, and he told me he did not speak to his parents for his entire first year on the road. I told him I could accept his decision, but I also wished that he had developed a better relationship with his parents. He said that sometimes he wished for that too.

"So." I said, "let's talk about the road." He told me that the show spent a little more than the original plan of a couple of months in Miami. In fact, they stayed booked into this club for four months while they worked out the logistics of the road schedule. "However, I did not stay with my friend for long." "Ok," I said, "What did you do?" "Well, shortly after the show opened in the Miami club, I began a relationship with a female bartender." "Is that so" I said. "I know. Can you believe it" "It was my first real relationship, and I felt like I had died and gone to heaven. This bartender was beautiful, smart, and financially successful."

"She had a master's degree in mathematics and a second degree in business." "I was clearly out of my league with this one." "Well," I said. "She must have seen something in you that appealed to her." "I agree," he said, "But I'm sure it had nothing to do with my math skills or business acumen." He just smiled at me. It was most refreshing since I rarely saw him smile. He continued to say that shortly after their relationship began. She asked him to move in with her and stay for as long as he was going to be in Miami. "There was no way I was going to turn that down." He said. I just said that I understood. I was young once myself.

Following the time to complete the road logistics, Chase told me they headed out of Miami and headed north to Maine of all places. "It was eight cars, an equipment truck, a star, a road manager, and our future which lay ahead." "I could not have been more excited and a little sad that I could not share my joy with my family." "Of course, He said, "The best laid plans of mice and men." I said. "I get the reference, so what about those plans?" He told me that for starters, the equipment truck broke down just after entering the New Jersey Turnpike. It was a U-Haul truck rental, so some of the band went ahead and called U-Haul for service. They returned and told us that the local U-Haul store said they could not come on to the Turnpike and administer service, because of a state contract with another towing company. I said, "What are we supposed to do?" "We can't afford to take this truck out of service, we will be so late for our first job in Maine." Our keyboard player said that we should contact the towing company that does have a contract with the Turnpike and make them take the truck to the local U-Haul store. " We said that was a great idea. Then I said, "Why don't a couple of us stay here with the truck and the rest of the band can go on. We will catch up with you as soon as possible. "So, a couple of us stayed with the truck until the towing company showed up. Then we would go with them to the U-Haul store and get the truck fixed" "Great plan,. Right" "Sounds good to me, very responsible." "You would think so, but fates had a different idea in mind.

"Before the band left, they went to the nearby plaza, found a phone and called the Turnpike Towing company." "We waited almost three hours for the tow truck to show up!"

"The only positive experience that day was that I wrote a new song called: *Stuck on the New Jersey Turnpike Blues.*" I laughed, "Do you still remember the song?" Chase just looked at me. "Of course, by the time we got to the U-Haul store, they were closed." "I was beside myself thinking, we are going to lose this job. A great way to start our road trip." Chase told me that while he was looking through the glass window of the store, he noticed a sticker that had the phone number of U-Hall corporate offices. He decided to try and call them, because U- Haul was supposed to have a 24-hour breakdown service. They were located in Texas and would probably still be open. So, he went to the corner and found a public phone and call U-Haul. "Thank God they answered." I was so into this story by now, I didn't even notice my session clock had indicated that our session was over." "I wasn't about to end this session before I found out what happened." Chase told me that a woman answered the phone and heard this crazy story from a musician out of Florida, who was almost hysterical.

He reminded her about the 24-hour service policy for rental vehicles, and that the repair facility appeared closed. She said, "Please hold on a minute ." Then according to Chase a male voice came on the phone and said, "This is Bob Thompson, President of U-Haul, How can I be of service?" By now, I was a believer in fate. Chase said he was floored. He told the President the whole story and when he was done, the President said, "Please give me the phone number you are calling from. "I gave him the number, "Chase said, "And he told me a person would call me back in five minutes and solve my problem." I said, "I can't thank you enough." He said, "Please don't worry about a thing, just call me back and tell me when your truck is fixed." Chase said he promised that he would call back.

"The President said," Good, I expect that you will be using our vehicles a number of times in the future, and I don't want to lose you as a customer."

Chase told me that their truck was repaired a couple of hours later, and they were on the road again. I said, "What a story, and what a life." Chase said, "Yeah, it was pretty cool." "We arrived at the hotel a few hours later than we were supposed to be there, but once we described what happened, management was fine." They said management told them to get some sleep and we would load in the next morning. We were not about to argue that decision.

CHAPTER NINE
THE LONG ROAD HOME

In our next session, Chase told me that after almost five years on the road, he was ready for new challenges. "Although I still loved the road, I desired a change and a fresh challenge." I toured the country, met incredible people, had more experiences with women than I could have ever imagined." "I was a responsible person, an adult." I said. "You grew up, and experienced more than most people did in a lifetime."

"One thing I was most proud of was a consistent pattern of success wherever we performed." I said, "You should be proud of that." "Yes, I am," he said. "And, as a group, we never did drugs, rarely drank alcohol, and did nothing to embarrass ourselves, the show, or any establishment in which we performed." "That is quite a record," I said. "It was, and as much as I enjoyed the road, I knew when it was time to get off." Chase told me that when summer came and they returned to Florida for one last job, and a well-deserve vacation. He informed management that he would not be returning. "It was bittersweet," he said, "But it was time to go"

I told Chase that it seemed like his overall road experience was a very positive one. He agreed, but then he related the underlying story I did not know of, or even a hint of, how it would profoundly affect him and his future.

Just as I thought we had made great strides with Chase; another tragedy was waiting in the wings. When he came in for his next session, I thought we were going to recap his road experiences and move on to the next segment in his life. As I have learned, nothing good ever lasts in the Chase world. Following our usual greetings and tea, I asked Chase where were we going today. It seemed logical, as one segment of his life had ended. He started out this way, "I am a cheat and I beg your forgiveness." I asked him what was he referring to. "I led you to believe," he said, "that my experience on the road was the only thing on my mind." "It wasn't, I said." "Not quite, and if you will indulge me, I will reveal the next scenario." I said, "Please continue." "When I first got the call to audition for this show, it wasn't a random call, but a recommendation from one of the show members. Scott, one of the horn players, who knew me and was aware that I was looking for road experience. He found out from a mutual friend we had gone to school with, and they provided my phone number to Scott, who turned it over to the management team, along with his recommendation. When I showed up at the audition, I was happy to see Scott. After the audition, when they told me I got the job for the show, Scott mentioned he planned to host a barbecue at his parents' home in Davie.

I said I would absolutely be there. The night of the party/barbecue, all the show members were there as well as other friends, including Scott and my mutual friend. I also met one more friend of Scott's. Her name was Kris. As the night wore on, I looked at Kris, and engaged her in conversation. She told me she was an old family friend who went to school with Scott. I could not help myself as I engaged her most of the night in conversation.

She seemed right at home talking to me and by the end of the night I was hooked. I found her beautiful and quirky and fun and just delightful.

However, I pursued nothing with her that night. That was probably the right course of action because, later on, my friend from school told me that Kris was more than just a family friend to Scott. In their circle of friends, they all went to school together, and they believed Scott would eventually end up with her. She was his girlfriend. I let the matter drop, but I never forgot Kris. I could tell by the way Chase was telling this story that it was going to get very complicated. Chase continued to say that during a break of the show's first year, the show returned home for a vacation. "I of course," said Chase, "had no place to stay. Scott's family, who were darling people, asked me if I wanted to stay with them. They had an RV on their considerable property, and they offered it to me whenever the show was in town. I accepted their offer and thanked them for their kindness. By this time, Scott and I were becoming great friends. I noted I could see where this might be going. Chase continued, "While we were on break, and while I was at Scott's farm in the RV, inevitably, I would run into Kris again when she visited the family. I was once again becoming seriously attracted to her, to where I knew I had to do something." Chase related to me that while on the road, he had written original songs, hoping to get a recording contract in the future. While not even consciously thinking about it," Chase said, "I found I had written a song for Kris." "During one of her visits, I asked her into my RV." "She said yes, and I found the chance to speak with her about my feelings." I remarked, "Didn't you think that might have been inappropriate since she was supposed to be Scott's girlfriend?"

Chase said, "I didn't really think about the consequences, I just acted on pure emotions." I said, "I can see how this could have been a major issue between Scott and you." "Point taken" he said, "but I was operating under the motivation of what I now know was love." "Ok, I said," "Now you've got her in the RV, which belonged to the parents of your show mate, who was supposed to be her boyfriend." "Are you sensing the potential problem here?" Chase said, "Of course I do, but I had no choice but to tell her how I felt." "I played and sang the song for her and when it was over, I told her I was pretty sure I was in love with her." Chase said, "I then waited for the fallout, but it never came." "She smiled, told me she loved the song, and then I kissed her." "Wow," I said. "That was bold, wasn't it?" "I don't know," he said, "It just seemed the natural thing to do." Chase said, "I then wanted to broach the subject of her relationship with Scott." "I have been told by others that you are in a relationship with Scott. If this is true, then I will back off, but you need to know how I feel." "I don't know what you've been told," Kris said, "or who told it to you, but Scott and I are just good friends." "Sure we hung out together, but that was with all our group of friends." "Scott has never told me he loved me, nor have I said that to him." "We are just good friends." I noted that Chase, even in our conversations today, had a different demeanor when talking about Kris. I knew that no matter how many years had gone by, this feeling that Chase had for Kris would never end. I told Chase that our session was over, and we would pick this up next time. He agreed and left, wishing me well.

CHAPTER TEN
ALL IS NOT FAIR IN LOVE

As our next session began, I told Chase that he should never be afraid to say anything to me, and I would always be on his side. "Well," Chase said, "I told Kris that I had to tell Scott how I felt about her.

We are going back on the road in a few days, and he and I are roommates this time out." "I have to tell him, just in case he still has romantic feelings for you, even though he may never have directly said as much to you." "I would not feel comfortable not telling him." Chase told me he and Kris both agreed it was the best course of action. Chase said to me, "I could have considered nothing more difficult to do." "If I could have, I would have quit the road that night." "But you and I understand commitment and the responsibility that goes along with it." I said I did, and I couldn't help thinking that Chase's sanctity of the word commitment would reappear as part of his operational toolkit in the future. At our next meeting, Chase told me he was very apprehensive and nervous about speaking to Scott about Kris. I told him I indeed supported his decision to speak to Scott, but that he should be sure that Kris was the one. Otherwise, I said, you might have put your friendship with Scott in danger, and if it didn't work out with Kris, you would have lost on two fronts.' Doc, please hear my heart on this. I have been with several women in this last year and a half while on the road." "And, as modesty permits, many of them were amazing women." But I have never been in Love." "I mean really in love. The love that messes with your thinking all the time." I asked if he wanted this to happen and, was he all right with the potential outcome? He said, "To be honest with you, I don't know." "I only know that all of my unoccupied time is now being spent thinking about Kris," "I know you said that you told Kris that you loved her." "Did that change your behavior on the road?" Chased stood up for a minute, collected his thoughts and then said, "I need you to understand something. When I told Kris I loved her, I had said nothing even remotely like that to anybody else, because those words represented a commitment to me." I thought, there is that commitment word again. I truly believed that Chase was very "old fashioned" for matters of the heart. I reassured him I completely understood the concept of a commitment, and I would never question his actions for romance. He said, "thank you." "So, what remained was how to tell Scott, correct?" "Yes," he said, "and it was one of the most difficult things I ever had to do." "I knew in my mind that Chase was being one hundred percent sincere, and part of me wanted to skip this next section. But I knew I couldn't. I feel the need to say something so that you will understand the relationship Chase and I had. For almost a year, I had lived vicariously through Chase and his experiences. I probably understood him better than any other person in the world. You must also understand the empathy I had developed during our relationship together. So when Chase told me how difficult this would be, I knew he wasn't blowing smoke my way. Considering how Chase has managed stressful situations in the past, I gave him a lot of latitude when he finally told me his story. I also increased my supply of tissues. Before we go for the day, I want to ask you a very personal question and please feel free to tell me to buzz off if you don't want to discuss it. Chase said, "Doc, we have already been through so much that I don't believe that there is anything you could ask me, that I would not be willing to answer." "Just the same." I said, I always want you to have the freedom to tell me when I am "Out of bounds." He said, if that time ever came, he would tell me immediately. I said that was fair enough. "So," Chase said, "What do you want to ask me that you feel I might not want to answer." I took a deep breath and said, "Knowing your early history and the incredible challenges you have faced in your lifetime, did you think it was fair to involve Kris in your anything but normal lifestyle?" "You know," he said, "All is not fair in love." I knew the challenges that I faced with Kris." "I also knew that old idiom 'The heart wants what it wants.'" Isn't that a bit childish?" I said. "Possibly so, but I was in love, for the first time in my life I was in love." "And I was not about to let Kris get away if at all possible." "OK," I said, "But you must admit that her lifestyle and yours at this time were miles apart." " She had a job, a career if you will, and so did you." "So did you think far enough ahead to answer the question, 'What happens after I tell Scott?"

"No," he said," I was pretty occupied on just the telling Scott part. I will admit that I didn't have a great plan." "I would say you didn't have any plan at all." "Doc, don't hurt me." "You may be right, but The heart wants what it wants." "That's so Chase" I said. He said, "Did I answer your question?" "Not really," I said, "But I am not willing to run this around the block and further." "Well," I said, "you certainly have a way of adding complications to the simplest of events." "I can hardly wait for the next chapter in your life," "Have a momentous week, and I will see you next time." I noted as he left, Chase did not have the same smile that he had just a brief time ago. I wondered what the next installment of his life would show me.

CHAPTER ELEVEN
WHY IS LIFE SO COMPLICATED?

When Chase came in for our next session, I offered him a cup of tea. I said, "Before we begin, let's just have a cup of tea and talk a bit." Chase said he was fine with that and was ready to talk about anything. I said that would be fine and we would get to the session in short order. As we were enjoying our tea, I said, "Chase, I was contacted by your daughter a couple of days ago." "What did she want," he said. I told him she has tried to stay away during this process but had the feeling that this was going to go on for a long time, and she wondered if it would be possible to get an update every so often. "Chase," "Do you want me talking to your daughter about our sessions?" "I know that I told you these sessions were private and not generally available to outside individuals." "You should know that I told her the very same thing, to which she seemed very sad and just a bit angry." "Chase, do you want me to speak directly to your daughter concerning our sessions."

Chase thought for a long while and asked, "Would you have to tell her everything, or could you be selective?" "Chase, I can be as selective as you want me to be." "I have no problem telling her a lot, or a little. Or, if it is you wishes, I will tell her nothing." "Doc," he said, "I don't know what the right answer is here." "Chase," I said, "There are no right or wrong answers, only what you want." "You control the mix." "This is your life, and nobody can dictate what you should do with it." "Comforting words Doc, But my daughter is still out in the cold with regard to me and our relationship." "I understand what you have said, maybe more than you know." "But at the end of the day, it is still your life and you are free to do with it whatever you want," And. I don't want to sound like a broken record, but perhaps, some things are better left unsaid," "Alright" I said, "I will speak to her, and tell her I am sorry but your sessions must remain private," "Doc, Please let me speak to her first. I will visit her this weekend and try to explain my position, I am sure she will understand." "Chase, that is a perfect response to a problem situation." " I will always carry out your wishes whenever I am made aware of them." "I am sorry to take up so much time on this subject, but I thought it was important." Doc," he said, "You have been a great therapist and a great friend, and I know you would never hurt me. "It isn't that I don't want family members to know what is going on in my life, but I have been experiencing parts of my life that I barely remember, and I don't quite know how to handle that." "Chase, I totally understand your position, but don't lose who you are in favor of what you are." And with that," I said, "can we get back to the story now?" Chase said," "Hey, I am not the one who asked for the breakout session." "I know it is my fault, please forgive me and let's start again." "You were just about to return to the road with your newfound information that Kris loved you, and you had to find a way to tell Scott." "Does that pretty much sum it up?" "Yes," Chase said, "You are good… I said, "It's a gift."

But the truth was that I knew that Chase would have a tough time explaining to Scott, how he was going to be any better for her than he was." After all, they were both on the road, playing out the new contract, while Kris was at home alone. And, although I know the phrase

"Absence makes the heart grow fonder," I always consider that line to be a bit naïve.

Sometimes, absence can make the heart go wander. I didn't want to see Chase lose to Kris, and I hoped that they could work out their struggles. Chase said he was able to see Kris before the show left town. He told me that they confirmed to each other that they loved each other and would remain strong during the remainder of the road contract. I felt a bit more comfortable hearing what Chase had to say.

CHAPTER TWELVE
THE TRUE MEASURE OF FRIENDSHIP

"Our next stop was Agusta Georgia, an interesting town," Chase said. The supper club that booked our show was huge, with an elevated stage and, of course, a lit dance floor." "Between our shows, the band played dance music." Chase told me he actually loved the "dance-band" feature of the show because he got to sing lead on several songs. "My second passion after playing guitar," Chase said, "was singing." I said I didn't know you sang as well as played the guitar, other than the one time you had related the event when you were twelve. Chase said, "hey, I'm a multi-talented guy." Then he smiled. "Ok" I said, "So now you are back on the road." "Did the thought ever occur to you to end the road experience and stay with Kris." "It did," he said, "But this year's performance commitment was for 18 months, and I agreed to it." "I know," I said, "you don't have to say it, commitment right." Chase just looked at me and we both knew. I must say, he was a principled guy. However, I didn't know how he was going to survive eighteen months without Kris.

So I said, "Chase, do you feel comfortable speaking about your discussion with Scott over you and Kris?" He said, "Comfort would never enter this discussion. I knew I had to do it; I was just looking for the right time." "Then, I realized that there would never be a right time. "I remember calling Kris and telling her I was going to tell Scott that night after the show."

"What was her response to that?" I asked. He said she told him to please be kind. She cared a lot about Scott and didn't want him to be hurt. "I told her," Chase said, "That if Scott considered Kris to be the one girl in his future, he was going to be hurt. But I would try my best to be as kind as possible." Chase told me that Kris asked him to please call her after it was over, no matter what the time. As I settled in to hear the next critical part, I buzzed my secretary and told her under no circumstances was she to interrupt me, for any reason. "Ok Chase," I said, "Whenever you are ready."

"We had a great show that night." Chase began, "We were exhausted, and the crowds were great, giving us a standing ovation at the end of the night." "As we walked back to our room, I asked Scott if he wanted to go out and get some breakfast." He told me the band often did this after a great show, since management usually bought. "No," Scott said, "I think I will just relax tonight." Chase said, "Do you mind if I hang with you? I'm kind of tired." Scott replied, "Absolutely." I sensed that the stage was now set for heart to heart. Chase then told me the entire story. "After we changed out of our show clothes into more comfortable attire, I offered Scott a coke, his favorite drink, he gratefully accepted. I had a diet coke myself." "After about ten minutes, I said to Scott, I need to talk to you about something." Scott said, "Sure, what's this about?" "Scott, I want you to know that I consider you to be one of my closest friends. As a matter of fact, I feel closer to you than my brother." Scott said, "I am very fond of you as well, Chase." "You are one hell of a guitar player, a quality person, and I wouldn't want to room with anyone else in this show." Chase told me his whole body was beginning to shake. I told him that was a normal reaction for a person in a very stressful situation. Chase continued, "I need to tell you something I have been struggling with for weeks."

Chase said that Scott sat up on the bed and turned and faced him and said, "It's alright, you can stop struggling, I know what is going on with you and Kris."

Chase said that was too much for him to hear, he started crying and the only thing he could say to Scott was, "I'm so sorry." At the same time, Chase is relating the story to me. He is crying in front of me as well. I poured him a glass of water and made sure he had a box of tissues handy. "Chase," I said, "If you need a break…" 'No, I'm ok" he said. "I need to get this out." I said, "when you are ready."

I knew this was a difficult discussion for Chase. After all, he is talking to a person he could easily call a "Brother," about Kris, whom he thought might still live in Scott's heart. He was going to say he was in love with her, and she was in love with him. I had empathy for the hurt that Chase was going through, but I knew he had to finish the story. I told Chase to continue whenever he was ready. We were over on the clock now, but I didn't care.

Chase said that Scott's statement surprised him and he needed to know more. "How long have you known?" Chase asked, Scott said. "For some time now. I didn't want to get involved just in case it was going to be short-lived," Chase replied. "I need to tell you I love Kris. I have told her so, and she has replied that she loves me too."

Finally,   I thought, It was out in the open and they could deal with it hopefully as friends. Scott said, "Oh, it's that serious." Chase said," Yes, I'm afraid so." Scott asked, "Why then did you consent to this road trip?" "I had already committed to management." Chase said, "And you know me and commitments." Scott said, "I understand." Chase then asked, "Are we going to get through this?" "Please tell me your feelings. I really need to know." Scott said, "First, I need to tell you I love Kris as well, but I love her as a friend. We grew up together, and I will always want what is best for her." "Are you what's best for her Chase?"

Chase said, "that single statement cut right through to my heart." "Was I the best person for Kris?" I had to stop Chase at this point and ask him if he was having second thoughts. Chase said, "Absolutely not. I felt strongly about Kris, and my dedication to her was unwavering.

I informed Scott that I had spent days contemplating whether I loved Kris. The only answer I could produce was yes, without a doubt." Scott then said, "Then I want you two to be in love forever and have a wonderful life." Chase replied, "That is all I want as well." "I hope you know I would do nothing to hurt Kris." "I am committed to her." "That is all I need to hear," Scott said. "You and I will be fine."

Chase told me that, "As the days and weeks rolled by, Scott and he remained good friends. I would never forget the night I told Scott and he basically blessed my relationship with Kris." With that conviction from Scott, Chase told me they could finally lay down months of stress and move forward. I said, "thank you for sharing your story. I know it was difficult." I knew Chase was finally comfortable sharing almost anything with me and he knew I would never hurt him. That, by far, was the longest and most gut-wrenching session of our entire relationship. I went home that night, fixed myself a potent drink, and tried to put the night out of my mind.

CHAPTER THIRTEEN
THE END OF AN ERA

Following that session, I didn't see Chase for almost a month. I called him to find out if anything was wrong. When I finally reached him, he said that he was sorry that he did not call me, but he felt he needed a break. I told him I understood that from time to time, patients need some space and an emotional holiday. I said I would be here whenever he was ready to come back. He thanked me and said he would be back soon.

I took the time away from Chase to have a brief holiday of my own. But even during my forced break, I could not help but think about Chase and what would be the next period he would want to talk about. I was beginning to really understand this very complicated individual, and yet, I still did not know what was driving his desire to re-live all the moments of his life at this time. Why couldn't he put the past aside and live for the moment?

He never seemed to want to talk about the present. I was concerned that he might lose touch with reality. I monitored his emotional state carefully when he returned for our sessions. I never for a moment thought he might not return. However, I could understand if these sessions were getting too difficult for him. I knew he didn't deserve the life he was being given. However, I did not know how terrible it was going to get. I waited with great anticipation for our next session to begin. I did not have to wait long.

My secretary told me that Chase had called and was ready to resume his sessions. She put him on the calendar for next week. I was relieved that

I hadn't lost a patient and a friend. I remembered the promise I made to myself to monitor closely Chase's behavior, especially his continuing emotional state.

The next time I saw Chase, I welcomed him back and offered him a cup of tea. "Just like always, right doc." "I am a creature of habit," I remarked. Chase just smiled, accepted the cup of tea with grace, and sat down. "I hope you are well." I said, "and that you are comfortable resuming our sessions." Chase said once again, "I am sorry for not telling you that needed a break." I said, "don't give it a second thought, you are always welcome here." He seemed grateful for the reassurance and as he finished his cup of tea, he stood up, took a deep breath, and said, "Let's get to it."

"Chase, where are we going to resume your story?" He took a minute and said, "I need to begin at the end of my era as a road musician." I said, "that seems like a great place to start today." He continued, "after fulfilling my agreement, I let show management know that when we returned to Florida, I would leave the show." "They said they would be sorry to lose me, but they understood."

Chase told me that by the time he was ready to leave the show, there were probably fifteen alumni members from the original lineup. I said that I didn't know there was such a turnover in the show's cast members. He said it was just an occupational hazard, and that many of the shows that they ran into repeatedly on the circuit had replaced members over the years. "Ok, so where are we now." I said. "We are back in Florida, and I am getting ready to move to Los Angeles." "Ok,"I said, "Now I need to have a conversation with you concerning your steadfast decision to move to Los Angeles." "Ok." Chase said, "let's get into this." I began, "You are now off the road, and back in Florida. You have Kris all to yourself." "My question is, wasn't that enough for you?" "Forgive me if I sound a bit crass but, for someone who has professed his undying love for another individual, who was now right next to him. Someone you could not see your life without, why would you choose to leave her alone again?" "Doc, I completely understand the question, and make no mistake, Kris and I discussed this for weeks, and she finally decided to let me go to LA because she knew that if I didn't, I would always wonder how successful I could have been." "In addition, I had gotten to the point where I hated Florida and felt it had nothing to offer me other than Kris." "I wanted more than anything for Kris to go with me." "She told me that she had commitments of her own in Florida and couldn't leave anytime in the near future," "OK. I can understand your position, but it truly seemed to me that you were willing to bet on Kris keeping her word to you, while you went off to find your future someplace else."

"I think you were playing a very dangerous relationship game my friend, and that is all I want to say on that subject." Chase thanked me for my honesty and I waited for the other proverbial shoe to drop. He said. "I was going to drive there and try as best as I could to get a recording contract. I was also anxious to do studio work in L.A." "In addition," he said, "I am going to get as many of my songs published and recorded by others." I said, "Sounds like a plan. Would you mind telling me where Kris was going to fit into this goal?" Chase told me they had discussed at great length his move to L.A. Kris knew Chase had to try his best to succeed, if they were ever to have a life together. "I felt confident that our relationship could withstand another period of separation." I thought to myself that this was a very naïve position to take, and I was concerned that he was going to tell me in the not-too- distant future that he and Kris had broken up. I knew that this would have a disastrous effect on his emotional state. I had to ask him, "Chase, did you really think this move through before deciding to go? He replied, "I did, and I knew there was a risk, but I felt that this might be my last opportunity to succeed in the music business." "I also knew that I was not willing to accept what a failure in L.A. might do to our relationship."

I told Chase that I understood his reasoning but considering how long he had already been apart from Kris, I was concerned that their relationship might not survive this new move. He told me he understood the risk, but he still felt he needed to go. He reminded me that they were still a relatively young couple, and they believed their love would survive. "There was also another factor that I haven't mentioned before." Ok, I thought, here we go again. Another Chase tragic moment is about to be revealed. I said, "Chase, you and I have been down this long winding road together for some time." "I know when you start out like this, it will not end well." "Go ahead , I'm listening." "Well," he said, "I knew that if I asked Kris to go to L.A." with me, her parents would not have been happy." "Wait, "he said, "no, that isn't even close." "Her parents would have exploded." "I knew they did not hold me in high regard, and I'm sure her father would have done whatever would be necessary to keep me from taking Kris to L.A." "I did not want to put Kris through that, so I took the high road." 'Did you ever talk to Kris about your relationship with her parents?" "Not really," he said. "But I knew she knew how they felt about me." "he said, I feared her father, and I knew that part of the driving force for me was to succeed at a high level, was so that he would at least tolerate me." I said. "Was this a genuine fear, or are you embellishing the situation?" "Oh no," he said. "My fear was genuine, and just the thought that he could eventually break us up was making me crazy." I said, "Do you really believe that he had that kind of hold on Kris?" Chase told me he felt Kris loved and respected her father, but he also felt that she was always under his thumb. "I did not realize it at first," he said," but the few times I was in their presence, I realized her father had a very domineering personality." "I truly felt that if I failed, I would be out of Kris's life in short order." "Wow," I said, "Chase you never fail to amaze me with the amount of challenges you had to face." "I will let this go for now, but trust me, Kris's father would play an important role in my future." I almost didn't want to hear how this would play out.

"So," Chase said, "win, loose, or draw, I was off the road and on my way to Los Angeles to start a new era." "Oh, by the way, I was originally counting on Scott to watch over Kris while I was gone. I felt safe asking him, and I knew Kris was still comfortable around him." "Well," I said, "that doesn't seem like a terrible idea." "I didn't think so either," said Chase. "Except, Scott announced he was going to drive to Los Angeles with me." I said, "It just keeps getting better and better." But I knew it was just part of the course in the Chase Roman world. I could hardly wait for the next episode. I escorted Chase out and told him I looked forward to our next session.

CHAPTER FOURTEEN
THE NEW WORLD

During our next session, Chase seemed happy to talk about his time in L.A. "L.A. was a fantastic place, full of music and entertainment. "I could join the Musicians union local number 47, so I could work at the studios." "Was it everything you expected it to be?" I asked. "It was certainly busy and very competitive." "There was more work that I could have ever imagined." "So, I asked, how did you spend your time?" "Well Scott stayed for a couple of weeks, and then he returned to Florida." "I asked him to be sure and check in on Kris, and he said he would." "After a short period, my parents (remember them) decided they were going to move to L.A." "How did that make you feel?" I asked. "Well," he said, "despite our estrangement, I was actually looking forward to seeing them."

My mom told me they had purchased a few businesses and a house in the Valley. They wanted me to move in. "It is an enormous house, and we are gone most of the day." "Did you do it," I asked. "Well," he said, it was free room and board, and as long as they didn't disturb me, I would take a shot."

"I think I remember Kris telling me she thought that was cute." "I also remember thinking was she making fun of me, or did she really think it was a good idea." "Did it really matter" I asked, "No, not really." I asked Chase how it was going with Kris and had he had changed his mind about their long-distance relationship. He told me not at all, but he was sorry he could not share his accomplishment with her. "I knew in the back of my mind that I had to see her soon, but she was teaching and her free time was limited." I said, "that's what happens sometimes in long-distance relationships. Each person still has to live their lives." Chase told me he understood that, but it was still difficult.

After about a year, Chase enrolled in the American Academy of Dramatic Arts in Pasadena. When he wasn't taking a union music job, or working in an L.A. studio, he thought acting might be one of his creative outlets. I said, "I didn't know you had the acting bug." He told me he had taken acting classes when he was in college and liked it very much, but the music thing came calling. I said. I knew you were eclectic, but it seems like you were becoming a Renaissance person. He just laughed. "However," he said, "The fact that I attended that school would play an important role in my future." I said, "Care to elaborate." Chase had told me the entire procedure to get into the Academy was grueling. "I had to audition three times in front of different people with different script sections that I had to learn." "Please don't get me wrong, I knew that the craft of acting was tough and people went for years without any success." "But I never thought that trying to get in to study the craft would be so difficult.

"I thought of walking away a few times, but then what would I lose?" I said to Chase, "I am very familiar with the Academy, Both in New York and in Pasadena." Chase said, "Why would you know anything about that place?" "What," I said, "you don't think that actors need a therapist from time to time." He said, "Really, you really were a therapist to some of those acting students?" Chase's eyes began to light up. I couldn't leave him hanging. "No, I had a cousin who attended the one in New

York City." "But it was great seeing your expression even just for a minute." I started to laugh and Chase said. "Doc, you are an evil, evil, man." "Yes, I am." And with that, we both laughed. "However, I want you to know that I have counselled a number of actors, including so very famous ones." "Doc," he said. "I have no doubt that you did."

"So, you really decided that if you got into the Academy, you would accept the program?" "Yes, I would," "What happened?" Chase told me that after a few more auditions and some interviews with some serious people, they let him in. "I was ecstatic." "The whole campus of the school was electric."

"There was always something going on, both at the school and off campus." "We had a huge bulletin board that displayed all the available professional acting auditions." "And, whenever any of my class got a part, we would all celebrate." "It was a wonderful time of camaraderie and expression," "But, it was also a time of sadness for me, because I had no one to share my incredible adventure with." "Missing Kris was beginning to take a real toll on my emotions." "I knew that I could not keep up this long-distance relationship much longer." "Chase, I know that you went to LA to seek out some fame and fortune." But did you ever think you made the wrong decision?" "To tell you the truth Doc, many times during the first year I was out there." "But I knew I had to at least try my best to succeed." "Ok, so you went there, you did some things, you had some great experiences, and what did you decide?" "I decided that I needed to talk to Kris about how we could survive this period in our lives'" I said, "I think that was a very positive and adult thing to do." "What did she say?" Chase told me that after his conversation with Kris, he felt he could finally work out a plan for her to visit him in L.A. She would try to come around Valentine's day, and again at Easter. "I was so excited to see her. I knew she loved to dance; she had studied jazz dance in college. My background was in music, not dance." He told me that dance was part of the curriculum at the Academy, and he enjoyed the classes. But he wanted to impress Kris, so he took classes at the local discotheque. After all, it was the Disco era. "When she finally arrived the first time in L.A. I was visibly stunned at how beautiful she was.," he said, "I could not keep my hands off her." "We went to dinner, and then I suggested we go to a local disco." "She agreed, and after we entered and got a drink, I said would you like to dance?" Chase told me she gave him the strangest look but agreed. "Once on the dance floor," he said, "A huge smile came across her face as she realized I could actually dance." After a few hours of dancing, we were exhausted, Chase told me. We went back to the hotel. That night, it was like discovering each other again. We made love until the morning. "I remember thinking," he said, "How am I ever going to let her go back to Florida?" "But she did, reminding me she would be back at Easter, and making him promise her they could go dancing again."

"I remember being so sad for a week." I said, "that too is part of the long-distance relationship." He told me that during that week when he had to go to class at the Academy, they were doing improv using music and any song the student wanted, but it had to be sung without music. "I started singing Barry Manilow's Weekend In New England, and halfway through the song I started crying." "I had to leave the class." "Wow," I said, "Kris was really doing a number on your emotional stability." He said, "You do not know how she affected me," "I knew I could not continue without her," I asked him what he thought was going to happen when Kris came at Easter. He told me he was going to ask her to move to L.A.

During their Easter visit, Chase told me that Kris was upset because she wanted to attend Miami University in Oxford, Ohio in order to seek her Doctorate Degree. But they said she was too young. "Did you know she wanted to do that? "I asked." "I did not know," he said. "But this was an important decision." "How could I ask to come and live with me." "When she left that weekend, I was devastated, but I did not say anything to her. How could I destroy her dream of earning this degree? I did not know what I was going to do. Part of me was sure that our relationship was over." Oh, Chase," I said, "I am sorry for what you must have been going through." Before our session was over, I felt the need to address some things with Chase. "Chase," I said. "I feel the need to go over your time in LA for just a little while longer, if you don't mind." "Doc," he said, "I knew this was going to happen." "We don't have to do this, if you would rather not." "Look, I know that going to LA might not have been the best move for my relationship with Kris. I mentioned that we had discussed this at great length when I was in Florida." "I do remember you saying something about that, But you really didn't know anything about L.A. or how it might affect you." Chase seemed to squirm a bit during this part of our conversation. I had the sinking feeling that there was something that he was leaving out. To me, the numbers didn't line up. I had to find out what was truly Chase's motivation for going to L.A. I decided to table it for now, and let Chase think about it before our next session. Chase left with hardly saying a word to me. I didn't know if he was mad at me, or he sensed that I knew something wasn't exactly kosher about his reason for going to L.A.

I got very little sleep that week, as I kept on playing through my mind the words that Chase had used to describe his motivation for moving to L.A. What I didn't understand was his insistence that L.A. was the only place he could succeed. Certainly, Miami had some great studios in those days. There was a strong Musician's Union in Miami that supported the Cruise ship industry, and the hotels that hired union musicians all the time. As a songwriter, he could have just as easily gone to Nashville, home of many successful song writers. And, after a year in L.A., he never mentioned his songs at all in our conversations. Something just didn't fit, but for the life of me, I couldn't see it. I had to lay it down for now, I hadn't really slept in the last three days, and if I didn't stop, I was going to need therapy. For the first time in my life, I was dreading my next meeting with Chase, because I knew I had to confront him and get to the bottom of this mystery. I will tell you now that what I ultimately found out rocked me to the core.

As I waited for Chase to show up for his usual meeting, I was conflicted about how to go about confronting him, and it truly bothered me. Chase and I had spent more than a year together sharing his most intimate and painful moments. I believed that he was always a straight up guy who loved to tell the truth, because his truth was definitely stranger than fiction.

I also thought that I had invested enough of myself into Chase, so that we had a special understanding and strength. A kind of strength that allowed us to stand together against a world that loved to attack him. Was I wrong? Was I deceiving myself? Had I all of a sudden forgot how to read people and situations. My mind was racing a mile a minute, I couldn't find my center. I had to use some of my own relaxation techniques to calm down. After a few minutes, I felt more in control. I could not believe what Chase was capable of doing to me. How he had controlled my very stability. I knew I had to put an end to this today.

Chase was late getting to my office, he quietly apologized and sat down. "No tea?" he asked. I said "I'm so sorry, let me get you some right away. "Doc," he said, "I was just kidding, you don't have to make tea right now." I said, "I know that, but I think tea is called for at this moment in time." Chase was silent while we drank our tea, when he finished, I began."

"Chase, I feel compelled to explain to you how I am feeling at this moment." "Isn't this a bit of a role reversal." He said. "I know, but humor me, if it isn't too much trouble. "That last statement came out hard, and I didn't mean to say it that way." "That's ok Doc." "What is this all about?"

"Chase, you and I now have a history together, and I must tell you that I have thoroughly enjoyed every minute we have spent trying to understand what you are all about." "Doc," Chase said, "I am right there with you. I never thought when we first began this journey that anything would come of it. I just thought we would spend a couple of weeks together to satisfy my kids and that would be it." "But this, I never expected this….." he paused for a moment, and then said, "thank you." I thought to myself, and now I am going to endanger that wonderful

relationship we have spent so long building. What was I thinking…
"Chase, I sincerely appreciate your sentiment, and it is because of what we have developed that I feel I must ask you some probing questions about your time in L.A."

Chase didn't say anything, but I could tell that he was really feeling nervous. "I can see that I may have struck a nerve here. I want you to know that I am only asking these questions for clarification, and not really for anything else." "Then why ask them?" Chase remarked.

"I guess because certain elements of what you have said don't seem to quite add up for me." "And, you know me, always searching for the truth." I could tell now that by Chase's physical demeanor, he knew he had to engage with me.

"Look Doc, If it is all the same to you, I would like to skip this part of my life." "Chase," I said, "You have never shown any resistance to talking about the most painful parts of your life. Why now the hesitation?" He hesitated for a long period of time. I knew this was going to be difficult for him to get through. Then he looked up at me and with tears in his eyes and said, "Because I am ashamed of an incident that happened on the road, and why I never told you, or worse, never told Kris." "Chase, this happened so long ago, and you and Kris had your run." Yes Doc, but I still love Kris and if she knew this story, she might never want to speak with me again, and I just can't risk that." "Chase, you know that everything we cover in this office is confidential, and I would never violate that trust." "Why don't we go through this story step by step and see if we can find a way to cope with it." Chase agreed, took a deep breath, and began. "

It was about the halfway mark in my contract with the show. We were playing…I think someplace in New York. During that time, The Miss World contest was being held. It was kind of like the Miss Universe Contest is today." "To our good fortune, the contestants were staying at our hotel." "One night before the contest a few of them came in to see the show. Believe me when I say we had no trouble identifying them as contestants." "They were all beautiful and captured the room as they found their way to a table in front of the stage." "At the end of the show, they were applauding as loudly as any of the other audience members." "So, I was sure they enjoyed the show." "During the show, I couldn't help staring at one of the girls." "She was stunningly beautiful, and I said to myself, this girl could definitely win the contest, I would vote for her." "I knew I was looking at her, but from the stage, it was a distance to the table where they were sitting." "Following the show, we were coming off the stage on our way to our rooms." "The very girl that I couldn't seem to take my eyes off, came right up to me and said" "Can I talk to you for a minute?" "I said sure, what can I do for you." "She said she was a contestant in the Miss World contest being held at the arena." I said, "No, really?" "Please forgive me, but don't you think the boys in the band knew who you were the minute came into the room" "You are all so incredibly beautiful." "She kind of blushed a bit and said, "Thank you." I said, "You are blushing, that is so cute." "She laughed a bit." "Well," she said, "The girls and I decided you were just flat out gorgeous, and very talented," "I didn't know what to say, I just smiled." She said, "Now who's blushing." "I knew I had to come up and talk to you before one of them did." "Doc, I was in heaven as you might imagine." I told Chase that he was painting quite a picture. "Can, I buy you a drink?" I said. "No, contestants are not allowed to drink as long as we are in the competition." "Oh, sure, I understand." "But you can take me to breakfast and buy me some coffee." I said, "If you will wait here while I go to my room to change, I would be honored to take you to breakfast." "She agreed, and I was off to my room." "As I waited for the elevator, she came up behind me and said," "All the other girls have left, and I don't want to be here alone. Do you mind if I come up to your room and wait while you change?" "I said, please do. I wouldn't want you sitting down here by yourself in that dress." "She just laughed." "Well Doc, as you can imagine, we didn't get to breakfast that night. She was incredible, so alluring. I was clearly in over my head here." "But there was also something comfortable about her." "She was very easy to talk to, very intelligent, like the girl next door." "It was like having Mary Ann and Ginger at the same time."

I said, "Chase, you may not know this, but you have not stopped smiling since you began talking about……who? "Oh, sorry Doc, her name was Lisa, and as you can imagine it, she was Miss California in the contest," The pieces were just starting to come together for me, and I didn't think I was going to like what came next. "Ok Chase, continue, It's your show."

"Well Doc, she did not win the contest, but she did come in second, which as it turned out was great for me since the winner was whisked off to interviews, parties, and a jet trip to someplace else." "And why was this good for you?" "Because as it turned out we got to spend the week together." "So far, I don't see the problem." "Well, after the week, she said she thought we were a good fit, her words, not mine." "And she wanted to see if it would be possible to start a relationship together." "Chase," I said, "Were you actually considering two long-distance relationships?" "Doc, I didn't know what I was considering," But she was there in my arms and Kris was not." "Not to throw another dart at you, but what did Scott say?" "Doc, the general rule the guys in the band all agreed to was 'don't ask, don't tell'". "Oh, wasn't that convenient." "So, what did you do?" "I said yes, and we started a relationship. She in Riverside, just outside LA, and me on the road." For the first time in my relationship with Chase, I felt betrayed, and I was not happy. "Chase, for how long did this long-distance relationship number two go on. "A long time, Lisa would send me pictures of her modelling jobs along with some very sexy letters." "A few times when she was on location and it was near where we were playing, she would come for a visit." "Chase," "Don't say it Doc." I said, "What were you thinking?" I think I was shouting by now, and I have never done that in a session before, never. But I was just so upset. "Ok Chase, how does this all tie into why you told me you were too ashamed to tell me about this before?" I knew exactly what he was going to say, I have been in this game way too long not to see the signs. Even though I knew, I also knew that I had to let Chase tell me himself.

"Doc, I was coming to the end of my contract with the show. In a couple of weeks, we would once again be in Miami and my last playing job that was scheduled for four weeks." I told lisa, and she begged me to come to LA and be with her." I finally knew why Chase didn't want to tell me this story. I could sense another Chase tragic moment was just around the corner.

By now, I could see that Chase was about to lose it again, I threw him the box of tissues. "I knew," He said, that I am betraying Kris, but I told Lisa that I would come to LA to be with her." And then he lost it. I told him we needed a break, hell, I needed a break.

I got up to make some tea, the kind I had that had a calming influence on the person drinking it. I hoped it would work on Chase. I knew we were going to be here for a while.

When we came back together, I had to say a few things to Chase. "Chase, if you don't mind, I would like to start." He said to go ahead. Chase, I know this was a long time ago, but it still clearly bothers you. I cannot say that what you did was your right to do. Only you can make that statement. What I will say is we all must consider the consequences of our actions and accept what happens in the fallout." "You wanted Kris, your life would not be the same without her." "I remember those exact words coming out of your mouth." "Then you wanted Lisa, and you were willing to move to LA to get her, even though you knew ultimately what that would do to Kris." I have to be honest here my friend and tell you that there was no way this was going to work out well." Chase said, "Doc, I don't mean to interrupt you, and I do agree with you one hundred percent, but please let me finish this part of the story." "Then you can yell at me." I told Chase that I did not mean to yell at him, and I would not do it again. "I'm sorry Chase, please continue."

"Ok, Scott and I arrived in LA, and after a couple of weeks, Scott left." "I could not wait to get to get to Lisa."

"I had her address, and I thought I would not call her, but drive out to Riverside and surprise her." When I got to her house, I noticed her car in the driveway. "She had told me she was going to buy a new Porche, and there it was in the driveway." "The anticipation was huge and I was so excited to see her." "I went up to the door and rang the doorbell." "After a few seconds, she opened the door." "She was as beautiful as she was the last time I saw her, and I was speechless."

"Lisa looked at me and instead of jumping into my arms as I knew she would, she backed up and said, "Chase, what are you doing here?" I said, "I am here for you, don't you remember you asked me to come to L.A. and be with you?" I could see that Chase was about to lose it again. "Oh my God," Lisa said, "I didn't think that you would actually do it." "I said I would do it!" "Oh Chase, I am so sorry that you came all this way." Chase said, "From somewhere behind her he heard a voice say, "Honey, Who is at the door?" "Who is that?" Chase asked her. Lisa said, "That is my fiancé, I just got engaged two weeks ago." "I am so so sorry Chase, But I have to go." "And with that, she shut the door and it was over." By this time, Chase was almost non-functional. I just let him stay as long as he needed to, but this session was over. After a while, Chase left without saying a word to me. I thought, incredible, another Chase tragedy. I knew that reliving that memory for Chase was difficult. I could now understand why he was reluctant to share that with me, and most especially, I could understand why he would not want to share that with Kris. I knew I would see him again, but I couldn't help thinking, how much more could this person take before something disastrous happened.

CHAPTER FIFTEEN

REDEMPTION ALWAYS COMES WITH A COST

In our next session, I asked Chase if there was more he wanted to say about his time in L.A. or was it time to move on. He said we need to cover one more incident and then we would move on. I said OK whenever you are ready.

"After Lisa, I realized what a fool I had been. I was willing to sacrifice the one true love in my life for someone who I really didn't even know. I vowed never to do that again." I said, "Sounds like a true learning moment had occurred," "I decided." He said, "That I would never let Kris know about Lisa." "I put that period out of my life forever." "Ok Chase, I will let you let go of that time, and never bring it up again in our sessions." Chase said to me that he was sorry for letting me down as well, and I told him that this was long long ago, and I was not really a part of it. But I appreciated the apology "But Please don't put me through anything like that again. Whenever you are ready." I almost didn't remember where we left off.

Well to recap when Kris left at Easter," he said. "I knew I had to do something was or I would lose her." "Eventually, she would gain entrance into Miami University, and I would be powerless to stop her." "I also knew that if she went to Ohio, our relationship would end." "After completing The American Academy of Dramatic Arts program, I was waiting for entrance into UCLA, and their film directing program." "Again Chase, I'm so profoundly sorry that once again in your life, obstacles continued to derail your relationship with Kris." He knew I was being very sincere. "So," he said, "you can sense the problem that I was facing." I said, "without a doubt." So I asked him if there was a conceivable solution to this situation or was Kris was going to be out of the picture. "I knew I could never let her go." "But the situation would come to a crossroads much sooner than I expected." I said, "In what way did that happen?" "Kris unexpectedly came out to L.A. at the beginning of July." He said, "She told me that Miami University had decided to let her in to their Doctoral program." "It would begin in late August, and if all went well, end after two years." As if emotion overcame him during our session, he said, "I was stunned. I did not know what to say."

I asked him how did he resolve this heart-breaking moment? He said, "I decided to forgo UCLA and their Film Directing program and defer to the needs of the one I was totally in love with." Then after a minute of pause, he said, "I asked her to marry me." "understanding that I was willing to go with her to Miami University." "She looked at me somewhat stunned and said." "Yes!, yes of course I'll marry you." "Are you sure this is what you want?" I said, "You are what I want, and if I have to travel two thousand miles to have you, It's a small price to pay." "Well," she said, "You know I have to be there by late August, How are we going to manage a wedding and everything that goes along with it?" Chase said, "Give me a moment for me, I mean for us to consider our options." I asked, "Did you really have options?" He said, "I didn't at that moment, I was flying by the seat of my pants." "But I knew, from that moment on, whatever options we considered, we had to do it together." "Wow," I said, "I guess you really were in love."

The love displayed in songs and movies." "The real deal." He said,

"Nothing less. I was in it for the long haul." "I was ready to make a commitment to this woman," Well, I thought, there's that commitment word again. I asked Chase how he and Kris finally worked out the logistics. "We would go to Las Vegas and get married," "Then, we would go back to Florida to see her parents and spend some time with them before we left for Ohio." "And Kris was alright with this plan?" I asked. "Yes, she was more than willing to work this out if it meant we would be together." I said, "You had some woman there my friend, and also, some issues to deal with." "I swear to God Chase, you can't just have a normal life, with normal people's problems."

"That wouldn't be my style." He said. I asked him how he felt about returning to Florida and to Kris's father and mother's house. He said it was just another obstacle to overcome. I thought, you are a brave soul, and I hoped it wouldn't all blow up in your face. So, according to Chase, he, and Kris, along with his parents, who agreed to go as witnesses and for support, left for Vegas. And, in July 1977, they were married.

The next obstacle in this chain of events Chase told me about was the phone call Kris had to make to her parents. "You didn't think it would have been a good idea to let them know" before the wedding?" Chase said, "Doc, I'm no fool." "I wasn't about to let Kris talk to her dad before the wedding." I said, "Chase, I'm developing a whole new appreciation for your intellect." "How did they take the news?" "I don't know for sure," he said. "Kris wasn't offering a lot of information." "I think she left it to my imagination." "But, you know," he said. "We were now man and wife, and as far as I was concerned, I made a lifelong commitment to Kris." "And you know about.." I stopped him, "Yes, I know about you and the word commitment." Chase just laughed. "So," he said, we were off to Florida, and then to Ohio." I could hardly wait for the next episode in the life of Chase Roman.

CHAPTER SIXTEEN
NEW BEGINNINGS

I was eager to start the next session with Chase. I felt like I had been on a journey with him. I wanted to hear about his return to Florida as a married man, and how Kris's parents were going to manage their daughter's new husband. As Chase came into my office, I already had the tea brewing.

We sat down, drank our tea, and I recalled the important points from our last session. "Chase," I said, "I wanted to make sure you are ready to move on, and that there were no lingering issues concerning our last session." Chase told me that although the last session was a difficult one, he was indeed ready to move on." I told him I was ready as well.

"Well, we were now back in Florida and at Kris's parents' house," Chase said. "To say the reception was lukewarm is being kind." Chase told me that Kris's mother was upset that she could not attend her daughter's wedding with all the pomp and circumstance that befitted a woman of Southern roots. "During a quiet moment," Chase said, "when I could speak with Kris's mom alone. I told her she did not have to worry, and that I truly loved her daughter and that I would take care of her as long as I lived." Her mom said, "I appreciate you saying that, and I believe you are indeed in love with my daughter." "I also think that you are a good man, honest and kind." "But I do have my doubts." "You just rushed into this marriage, and now you are headed off to Ohio, where you will be alone." Chase told me he wanted to be totally honest with Kris's mom. "I can't tell you I'm not scared, or that everything is going to be perfect." "I know that is not likely." "But I also know the strength and commitment of Kris, and I have no doubts that she will be successful." "And what about you?," she asked. "Well," I said, "I don't know if I will get into Miami with just an Associate's Degree."

"I have given up an almost sure admittance into UCLA, because I love your daughter that much." "And I can't help but believe that I will make it work out." Kris's mom gave me a hug and said, "I sincerely hope so." "I am in your corner, but her father is another hill you are going to have to climb." I said, "And I know I have to climb that hill alone." I just smiled and walked away. I asked Chase why he thought Kris's father was so intractable. He told me Kris's father had almost planned out her whole life.

"I am convinced," he said, "that he wanted Kris to go to Miami University because that is where he received his Doctorate, and they would be the first father-daughter Doctorates from the same department." "She probably could have applied to UCLA or USC, both prestigious institutions, and I could have stayed at UCLA." "But that would not be an option as far as her father was concerned." So, I asked Chase if he always had an adversarial relationship with Kris's dad. He told me absolutely. "However," he said, "As strange as it sounds, he actually helped get me into Miami University," "He also provided off-campus housing for us." I said, "seemed like a friendly gesture." He said it was , but I shouldn't read a lot into that gesture. He believed that if Kris was to stay at Miami, then I would have to have at least a fighting chance at getting in as well. Otherwise, I'm sure he felt I would have convinced Kris to leave after the first year. And he said, "Although I was grateful that we had a place got to live, I knew that behind his altruistic gesture was another way to control us." It's not a side I'm used to seeing in you." Well," he said, this guy pushed all my wrong buttons, and I know the one thing he wanted most was to have Kris and me break up." "Wow," I said, "I did not know." "But you got in, didn't you?" "Yes," he said. "And that is another interesting story." "Yours always are" I said. "Ok, let's hear it." Chase just smiled. "When I met with my advisor in the Communications, Media, and Theater Department, we had a lengthy conversation." "After a while, I was thinking they would not accept me into the program." "After all, I only had an A.A. Degree, "And here I was, trying to get into the 18th ranked university in the nation, despite not having a communication or theater background." "Well," I said, "While in Los Angeles, I attended The American Academy of Dramatic Arts, and developed a great love and respect for actors and the craft." My advisor paused for a moment and then said, "Well, I'm impressed." "I will consider you, if you will do one thing for me." "I said, "I will do anything you ask, if it will help me get in." "ok" he said. "I want you to come to the theater tonight and audition for our first major stage production." "I take it you studied different vocal applications while at The Academy." I said, "I sure did." "Great, "he said, "And you can do an English or Scottish accent?" "Yes, I can." "Terrific, Then I will see you tonight." Chase told me he left the office and could not believe his great luck. "I never thought that my attendance at the Academy, based on just a whim I had one day, would have had a causal link to my getting in to this school." "It's Kismet," I said. "So, what happened at the audition?"

Chase told me he felt so strange walking into the theater department, not knowing anybody, and all the students there were auditioning for the show. It was customary for the seniors to get the major roles, as they needed the credit, and professional theater people would be there to see their work. "I did not know that." "I found that out later when I was in the department." "So, here I was trying to take a leading role away from a legitimate student, and I wasn't even part of the university yet."

"I got the part and was provisionally admitted to the Theater Department of this incredible school." I said, "Congratulations, and well done." "Yes," he said." Kris was so excited when I told her the news." "I knew you could do it!" she said. "I just smiled." "We went to dinner to celebrate and had such great sex that night." "Yeah," I said, "I could have done without that last part." Chase just smiled at me. He then told me about the incredible schedule he and Kris had set up for themselves. They would stay at the University all year and take as many classes as possible. Kris was determined to complete her Doctoral program in two years.

Chase said, "Kris had a free ride and an internship working for the Dean of the College of Education." "I on the other hand, had to pay for all my classes, and this was a very expensive private school. I had saved a significant amount of money, but I knew I was going to burn through it pretty quickly." "One bonus I took advantage of was the maximum credit fee structure."

"It meant that the University could only charge for up to fifteen course hours. Anything after that was free." "This worked out well for me since, according to our plan, I would have to take twenty hours a semester." "Wow," I said, "That seems to me to be a very difficult schedule to follow." "Tell me about it," Chase said. "But we were committed to getting this done, and we jumped into it with both feet." "After the first year, I completed my bachelor's degree, and must have impressed the establishment, because they accepted me into the Master's program and even offered me an internship." "That was quite an accomplishment," I said. "We did it," he confirmed.

"Kris and I completed our programs on time." She earned her Doctorate, and I completed my master's degree." "Quite impressive," I said. Chase agreed but took the time to tell me that the stress of it all took its toll on their relationship. "When it was all over," Chase said, "I said to Kris, You know if we could get jobs at this university, I would never leave." He told me that while she appreciated the sentiment, she wanted to return to South Florida. "In my heart of hearts," he said, "I knew this was a bad idea, but I agreed to go back to Florida. I sensed Chase was trying to tell me something. His facial expression seemed painful, and he was just staring at the ceiling. I assumed he was processing past information, but it would have to wait for our next session.

CHAPTER SEVENTEEN
THE BEST LAID PLANS….

When Chase returned for our next session, something in me triggered concern. His entire demeanor was off, and if I didn't know any better, I could have sworn he had been crying. "Are you alright Chase?" I asked. "You seem to be distant today."

"No, I'm alright" he said. "It's just that these sessions seem to influence me." "We can postpone, if you would rather." I said. "No," he replied, "I would like to continue." "Alright," I said, "Whenever you are ready." "Well," he began, "Kris and I were getting ready to return to South Florida, and her father and mother helped us move." I said, "That seemed like a friendly gesture." "I should mention that towards the end of my program., after Kris had already finished, she returned to Florida for a couple of weeks. When she returned, she mentioned her parents were coming to help us move and that her father had purchased a new double-wide mobile home for us to live in when we returned." Wow" I said, "Just like that." "In addition," she said, "I have taken a consultant job with the school district." "Well," I said, "Then it's all decided." I could tell just by looking at him that this part of Chase's life would not be good. I thought to myself, could this be the end of Camelot? "Well," he said, "Kris's parents showed up, and we while we were loading our possessions into the van, her father took the time to speak to me." "I want you to know" he said, "That I still believe that you are not good for my daughter." I have advised her that when you two return to Florida and work, that she keeps her finances separate from yours, just in case." Chase told me that in his mind he was thinking, "Just in case!, Just in case!. What the hell does that mean?" He said he didn't even respond to her father, worrying that he might take this to a level that he could never walk back. I knew he was hurting, and I was sorry that he had to relive these moments. I said, "let's take a break and have some tea." After a while, I asked Chase if he wanted to continue, or should we call it a day? He said," No, I need to get through this period, and then put it away." I said ok while thinking to myself, how does one person survive all this?

I was to find out that later that sometimes appeasement is just too high a price to pay. Chase began, "When we got back into Florida, I know my relationship with Kris had been strained." "I just didn't know how much damage had been done and could we survive?" Kris went to work for the school district and I got a job at a university in Boca Raton." "I thought we were doing ok and could move forward." "Nothing could be further from the truth." Even though I had a feeling about what was to come, I dreaded the thought of hearing it. "One day in the fall, Kris came up to me and told me she didn't want to be married anymore." "That she was tired of all the fighting and needed something new in her life." So there it was. I couldn't help but notice the tears that were coming from Chase, even though this was an event that happened so long ago.

I knew from years of practice that you can never truly get over your first love. So, I asked Chase, "What did you do?" "What could I do." "Kris wanted a divorce, and I couldn't argue with her." "Her speech seemed so clear, direct, and matter of fact." "As if she had been planning this for some time." Chase then said. "I told her, Kris, whatever you want me to do, I will do." He told me later that those words were the hardest words he ever had to say. Needless to say, he was crushed. I said, "Chase, again, I am so profoundly sorry for what you had to go through." He paused for a moment. Then he said, "Over the years, as I had time to try to understand what had happened between Kris and I, I could not for the life of me produce a good reason. "After all, we had just kicked each other's butts through one of the most grueling college programs anywhere." "And did it in record time." "Why couldn't that be enough?" "If anything, I thought the experience would have made us closer." Sometimes I told Chase, very stressful conditions can make people want to be by themselves and not have anything to do with the event or anyone connected to it." "But I was her husband!" "True," I said, "But you were also a co-member of the stress, and as long as you were around, Kris would be reminded of the event." "Doc, that sounds like spaghetti logic." "Did she just not love me enough?" I said to Chase to pull back a little and let's see the big picture.

I tried to explain that his circumstances were unique, not rare, just unique. I then asked," How long were you married before you left for Oxford?" "About two weeks." "So, Kris and you just went through one quasi stressful moment, and please understand., weddings are stressful no matter under what circumstances they take place, for another stressful moment." "Kris was about to start an incredible journey that many people much older than her try and fail to succeed." "And she planned to complete her program is two years as opposed to the normal four to five years that it normally takes to complete." "And at one of the toughest Universities in the nation." "Forgive me for saying this, but wonder woman was heading into the land of stress." Chase said, "I must agree, but she said she was ready for the challenge." "That in no way qualified her to avoid the unknown stress that waited for her." Now, let's take a look at your situation." "Oh boy," Chase said, "here it comes." "Here it comes indeed," I said. "You had agreed to go with her to a Major League University, to study a program for which you had little background." "You were coming from a minimum quality school, no offense, to a major institution of learning." "You probably suspected that you were in over your head, but you agreed, and an agreement is the same as a… Commitment." Chase said, "I knew you were going to find a way to throw that word into the mix." "None the less." I said, "and to add to the stress fest you were about to get into, you decided to take twenty college hours a semester, all year long" "Who does that." Nobel laureates. I told Chase that I am sure that in his wildest imagination, he could not foresee the level of stress he and Kris were about to undertake. "So please," I said, "Don't talk to me about stress, you and Kris invented the word." "I don't want to throw another log on the fire. But have you forgotten about Kris's father, who was just waiting in the wings to swoop in and save Kris once you ran yelling and screaming from Oxford." "Ok," Chase said, "I think I understand why Kris felt she had to leave." "But the amount of time I spent trying to figure this whole thing out, led me to a conclusion," "What conclusion, and how did you deal with it?" "I did not understand at the time, that Kris wanted me to come after her." "I guess to prove my love for her." With that statement, Chase broke down again. "I just never thought that I should stop her." "I didn't understand, Dam it! I just didn't understand!" "I could have kept her, If only I understood!" "What was wrong with me?" "Chase," I said,

"Please don't beat yourself up over something that happened so many years ago." "You are not a mind reader, and I know you felt blindsided by Kris's decision to leave you." "I know, but for years I asked myself, wasn't I good enough for her?" "For some time, I thought her father had convinced her that I was indeed not good enough for her," "I honestly believe," I said, "That none of those factors were what made Kris leave," "I believe that she had reached a dead end, and wanted, no needed a change, and you were just part of the fallout." "I am not sure, but even if you chased after her and caught her, she might not have come back." I don't know." "I don't know either." Chase said, "But I should have tried." "Chase, don't you think it is about time to lay this all down and forgive yourself?" "So many years of carrying that guilty cross, could not have been healthy." "I know Doc, and I am so exhausted" I decided to let Chase out of today's session with some hopefully helpful words. "Chase, I want you to go home and try to relax today and tonight." You deserve to be at peace with your circumstances." "Please remember that these sessions contain elements of your past, and not your future." "You can have any future you want; it is an open book. It is Just waiting for you to fill it up with new and exciting experiences." "For too long, you have been living in the past, feeling the same guilt you felt as a child at home." "Please allow me to give you permission to move on." "I even give you permission to remove the shame you felt when you were raped." "None of these experiences can lead to any emotional profitability, and I want you to be emotionally profitable." "Is there anything as a therapist that I can do for you so you don't carry this pain around with you even one more day?"

"Doc," he said, "You couldn't possibly say anything to me that would alter how I feel, even to this day." I said." Please know that I am here for you." As our session ended, I could tell that Chase was drained of all emotion. I realized he had never forgotten Kris and was still in love with her. I did not know what it was going to take to get him over this situation. I wouldn't have to wait long to find out that answer.

CHAPTER EIGHTEEN
LIFE AFTER...

It would be another two weeks before I saw Chase again. I had to attend a conference in Philadelphia, and though I needed to see Chase, I couldn't get out of this conference since I was one of the guest speakers. When I returned to my office, my secretary told me that Chase had called while I was away. When she told him I would be back next week, she sensed that although he said ok and he would be in for our next session; he seemed very sad. Now, I was regretting not cancelling my conference. I hoped Chase would forgive me. When he arrived, I offered him some tea and apologized for not being here when he needed me. He told me it was all right, but as he sat down, I knew he was still hurting. I said, "whenever you are ready, or we could just talk about stuff, if you would rather do that." He thanked me for my kind suggestion, but said he was ready to continue. During the next couple of hours, Chase told me about how unable he was to cope with Kris's decision to leave him. "I went to work each day like a ghost, preferring not to discuss my private life with any of my workmates." I told him that his behavior was neither unusual nor extreme considering what he had been through. I realized as I heard Chase speak, this pain was unlike any he had experienced before, and I knew he knew about pain.

"Chase," I said, "'What you are going through, including your profound sorrow, is understandable, but, if I may, not healthy in the long run." "I will help you though this stage in any way I can, if you will let me." Chase said, "Doc, I appreciate more than you know your desire to help me, especially since I have been carrying this around with me for over thirty years." "And I so appreciate your comments to me in our last session." "I want to be able to put this down and move on, I just don't know how at this moment in time."

"However, I know life does indeed go on, and as I have written in one of my songs, sometimes dreams don't come true, no matter what you do." I said, "Thank you for sharing that with me. You have coped with the pain." "Alright," I said," Let's travel back in time once more." "In the final days of my marriage, the only meetings I had with Kris were to discuss the terms of the divorce." "And each time I left her, I asked myself, What happened? What went wrong? Wasn't my love and support enough?" "Chase," I said, "sometimes life impedes happiness." "At best, we are all fragile human beings with built in coping mechanisms." "And sorry to say, sometimes love is not enough." "I don't know about the effect of life on love," he said, But I know the effect a father can have on relationships." "So," I said, you blamed Kris's father for your breakup?" "I don't know for sure, but he was certainly in the mix." "I think we need a break, let's get some tea." "you and your tea" Chase smiled," It was a smile I hadn't seen in quite a while. I was thankful for it. When we returned, Chase told me that following their breakup, he was in such terrible shape, he almost couldn't function on a day-to-day basis.

"After the final paperwork was done, I didn't see Kris again." "I will tell you how bad it got," Chase said. "I even moved back in with my parents, who had come back from California while I was in Oxford, Ohio. My dad had a heart attack and had mellowed quite a bit."

"Probably because he knew he needed my mother to care for him, so pissing her off was not a good idea." "I was just going through the motions of life, when a blessing from above stepped into my life." "After my separation from Kris, I didn't feel like playing much, so I didn't. One day, a musician friend called me from Nashville, where he was trying to get a record deal." "Evidently, that wasn't working out. So he was returning to South Florida, where he had played for so many years." "He asked if I would be interested in putting a band together and leading it when he returned." "He told me he already had work lined up and was ready to go into rehearsal." "Somehow, I didn't hesitate at all. I said I would do it." I told chase I was not surprised that he had accepted the position, reminding him of his former statement to me about music being the only staple in his life. He said, "You are so right."

"It was energizing for me to get back to music." "I felt myself sensing a new purpose, and I was for the first time in a long while excited to get up in the morning." I told Chase that I was proud of his decision to join humans again." As he left that day, I felt a little more at ease with his situation. I hoped our next session would be a pleasant one."

CHAPTER NINETEEN
A NEW CHANCE ENCOUNTER

Chase came in today and wanted to get right to the session. I knew better than to challenge him when he seemed this focused. Besides, I was eager to hear about this next section of his life story. "I want you to understand," Chase said, "That I was still reeling from the loss of Kris." "I don't think I will ever truly get over her." "But now," he said, "I could actually move my life forward in a positive direction." I told him I totally supported that decision. "I created the band that my friend from Nashville wanted.

His name was Arlo Smith, and he wanted a contemporary country band." "Now," he said, Country Music was not actually my wheelhouse, but after I listened to some songs Arlo wanted in his show, I thought this might be very cool." "About a third of his show included his original songs, the rest were songs by Kenny Rogers, Alabama, The Bellamy Brothers, Glen Campbell, and others." "I liked the music of most of these artists, and I thought to myself, I can do this." "Plus, I had assembled a killer band with serious musicians, most of whom I am still friends with today." I told Chase that he was working in the right direction, and this was a good start towards establishing his new life." Even as I said this to him, I wondered if he could put his never-ending feelings for Kris aside and give his full attention to this project."

I had to ask, "Chase, were you using this new project to move away from Kris?" "Well," he said, "that was not my primary motivation. I just wanted to play and be on stage again." "Although I must admit, after a year of performing and being with some very appealing women, I could forget how badly Kris had hurt me." "While she wasn't gone from my memory, I could put her in a very private area of my heart, and I was not about to let her hurt me again."

I told Chase that it appears that he had moved on, even if he didn't want to believe it. That statement about putting Kris in a special private part of his heart, to me, was code for "I am ok to move on without you." I knew he could never totally forget her, but he made the adult decision to move out from under her shadow. I believed he would be ok." I must admit that our next few sessions were actually boring. There was not much drama to discuss. I asked Chase if he thought we might wind down our sessions.

He told me, "Doc, there is a whole new world we are about to enter, and I'm sure I'm going to get my money's worth." I said, "wow, I can hardly wait." Part of me wondered what the heck he was talking about. I didn't have long to wait for the next shoe to drop. Following the next few weeks of Chase regaling me with his new connections and how I could never imagine how many women loved country music and the musicians who brought the sound to the stage, I had to say to him, "Chase, is it just possible that you were engaging in a process known as rebound relationships as a crutch to get over Kris?" "Doc" he said, "I don't know what it is called, but I was having a great deal of fun." I said to him, "you must have known that this would not last." "I know." He said, "but for the time being, it was a comfortable distraction." I said, "so was that going to be your permanent escape mechanism?" "I didn't know, but something was about to change me all over again."

CHAPTER TWENTY
JUST WHEN YOU LEAST EXPECT IT…

I had hoped that this somewhat adolescent behavior coming from Chase was going to run its course, and as usual, it did. In our next session, Chase came into the office and told me he was ready once again to consider a new relationship. I said, "do you mean now, or then?" He just laughed, and said, "No, I'm talking about the early nineteen eighties. "Alright," I said, "I have been waiting for this moment." "Let's get started."

Chase told me about a novel experience he had, and what was different about this new person. "I came in for practice one afternoon and I had a splitting headache." "I didn't have any aspirin, so I went to the bar to see if there was any available," As I rounded the corner, I saw her!" "She was incredible and I had to get closer to her."

Chase told me that this bartender had short white hair, and a tan that was to die for. I said, "So she made an impression on you?"

Chase said, "actually, I was mentally undressing her as I was walking to the bar." "Chase," I said, "Please keep it PG." Chase told me he wanted me to know the impact this person was having on him. "So," I said, "What did you do when you got to the bar?' "I said hello, and she said, "get away from me." "I was stunned!" "Excuse me, what have I done to deserve this attitude?" She said, "nothing, but you are Chase, right?" I said, "Yes, I am. Do I know you?" "No, she said, "but I know you." "or I know about you." I said, "What do you know about me?" "I know, "she said, that you have been through every female employee in this place."

"And, if everything these women are saying about you is true, then you are a legend around here." "And, quite frankly, I am not interested in being another one of your conquests." I said, "I don't know what these women are saying about me, but I can assure you that I am a gentleman." Chase told me that the bartender had just laughed at that statement and told him to move on. "Ok," I said, "so what happened next?" Chase said to me "You are really enjoying this, aren't you?" I said, "I'm just impressed that you would want to engage in conversation with this woman." "It seemed to be clear that she wanted nothing to do with you." "Yeah." He smiled, "I took it as a challenge" "Really," I said, "and what did you hope to gain from this challenge?" "Well, if nothing else, a date." I just laughed and said, "So which part of- get away from me-, did you not understand?" "Oh, I understood alright, but she was the first person in a very long time who had a profound effect on me, and I wasn't about to let this one get away, without a fight." I told Chase that someday, we needed to talk about interpersonal relationships. "alright, so now we are in it." "Where are we going from here?" Chase just smiled at me and said, "see you next week." As he was walking out the door, I said, "That's not fair" I could hear him laughing all the way to the elevator." The truth is, I was happy that he might have found a new significant relationship. I could hardly wait for our next session.

CHAPTER TWENTY–ONE
BE CAREFUL WHAT YOU WISH FOR…

As Chase came into my office, I said, "let's have some tea and slow this process down a bit" Chase agreed, and we drank tea and were quiet for a while. "Ok," I said, "Are you ready to move on?" Chase told me he was ready to discuss Amber. I said, "well, at least you got her name, that's progress." "Yes," he said, "But it wasn't easy." I told him that relationships that are worth developing are seldom easy. "So," he said, after a few weeks went by, and I thought Amber was never going to happen. I'm at the bar after our last set, and I see Amber talking to a customer."

"Somehow, I heard my name in the conversation, so I looked over to see the customer pointing at me." "Then, Amber smiled at me, and I knew I was in trouble." "What was that all about?' I asked. "I wasn't sure, until the customer got up to leave and as he passed by me, he said, "have fun." " I looked over at Amber and said, "why was I in the conversation, and what did that customer mean by, have fun?" Chase told me that Amber had told the customer that she had a date with him after closing. I said, "really?" She said, "alright calm down, we don't have to go out, but I would appreciate a ride home if it isn't too much trouble." I said, "No trouble at all. I will be packed up in a few minutes." I said that it seemed to me that Amber was having a change of heart. "Well," he said, "I think she just wanted a ride home." "So………" "So, we left together, and I had every intention of driving her home." "Somehow," I said, "I don't hear the sincerity in your voice." "Well," he said, "I asked her if she was hungry and did she want to have breakfast?" She said, "Um… I could eat." I said, "I think the die is cast here." Chase said it was just breakfast. I said, "Yeah, and J. Edgar Hoover never wore woman's clothing." Chase just smiled, and it was a devilish smile.

"Hours later, Chase said, as I'm walking to the bathroom in her condo, I ran into her roommate, who had come on to me in the past." "Bad timing was the only reason we never got together." "As I was in the bathroom, Amber's roommate went into her bedroom and said, "What is Chase doing here? I thought you wanted nothing to do with him." Chase said that he assumed that Amber just smiled, because her roommate passed me on the way back to her room laughing. "OK," I said, was this going to be a new relationship?" Chase Said it was, but it was not without its share of struggles. I wanted to hear lots more, but we were out of time. I told Chase that I wanted to hear all about this relationship in our next session. Chase agreed, but said, "Remember, you asked for this." As Chased left, I was thinking, maybe I didn't really want to know, but I asked, so I waited for next week to show up, with some doubts.

During our next session, Chase told me he was indeed pursuing a relationship with Amber. They went out several times. He met her family, including her five brothers. "I remember thinking." He said, "That I was pretty sure I could take them in a fight." "Amber and I were definitely an item, and my friends in the band were ready to embrace her." Chase told me they went out quite a bit, to the movies, or the mall, where they would spend way too much money." I said, "That too is part of a relationship." Chase said, "stop will you," I just smiled. After about a year, Chase said that one night Amber said, "Can I ask you a question, and I want you to be totally honest with me." Chase said, "sure I can be honest," I immediately thought to myself, this will not end well. "Tell me," Amber said, "When was the last time you were with another woman?" Oh boy, I thought, here it comes."

Chase thought about it for a minute, and then said, "Actually, last night." I thought, you are just a glutton for punishment. This is gonna cost you a lot of time. Chase said that Amber just got up, got dressed, and left. I said, "Well, what did you think she was going to do?" "I didn't know," he said, "After all, she asked me to be honest."

Chase told me that for the next few months, things were strained between them. I said, "No! I'm shocked," Chase said to me, "You know, you have a mean streak in you." "Anyway, I think Amber found a way to get back at me for being as she put it, 'A pompous ass." "Ok," I said, "I can hardly wait to hear how this went." "You know, I beginning to develop a definite liking for Amber." Chase just looked at me and gave me the "really" look.

Chase said, "Ok, it's just after the band finished, and I was moving to the bar to see Amber." "Her shift was over and I asked her to wait for me and I would take her to breakfast and then home." "As I approached the bar, she was having a drink and talking to one of her friends. I said hello and asked, "What are you drinking? I think she said a rum and coke." "would you like one?" I said, "Amber, you know I don't drink." "Oh yeah," she said, "Mr. fitness, who never consumes anything bad." I said, "That's not it, I just have never acquired the taste for alcohol, but if I were to drink, I smiled at her." She said, "Don't say anything you can't walk back." "Like what?" I said. Amber is trying to mimic Chase. "Like 'if I was a drinker, I bet I could drink you under the table'". I said, "You actually said that to Amber, a bartender." "I did." "Man," I said, "You were just asking for it." He chuckled. "Yes, I was, and there would never come a time in our relationship when I regretted that statement more than just at that moment." "What did Amber do?" Chase told me she got up and went behind the bar, placing empty glasses in front of me. " What's your poison." She asked. I said, I don't know, I'll leave it up to you." "Fair enough, White Russians all around." Chase said that he had seen a White Russian before and he thought he might like to try one." I laughed and said, "Oh, you were going to try more than one, I guarantee it."

He told me, as it turned out, he tried eight of them over the course of an hour. I said, and you didn't pass out?' Chase said, "you are enjoying this way too much. You don't even know what happened." "Oh, I know what happened alright."

"White Russians can make you blind." "Ok," Chase said, "So maybe I couldn't find my way out of the bar. And maybe I couldn't remember how I got home that night, or what happened to the three days that seemed to pass before I woke up." "Wow, you probably had alcohol poisoning." "You think," he said. "So, what happened next?" "Well, for starters, I said I will never speak to this woman again." "I will never have anything to do with her." "It's over. I never want to see her again." Chase told me that just then, his mom came into the room and said there was someone named Amber at the door and did he want to see her? "No, he said, absolutely not, tell her to go away and die somewhere." His mom said, "Really, she seems like a very nice person, and very pretty." Chase finally said, "All right, let her in, that way I can tell her to go and die somewhere." Chase told me that when Amber came into his room, she took one look at him and started laughing. "Very funny, "he said. She said to him, what was he complaining about, she had to get up and was pouring at the bar the next day at around ten in the morning. Chase said to her, "What are you doing here, did you come to gloat?" "No," she said. "Well maybe a little." "I tried calling you at work, and they told me you were sick and hadn't been in for three days." "Oh my god, I killed you I thought." "So, I had to come to see if you were still alive." "Barely," I said. "Are we ok? She asked. I said, "Not at this moment, but maybe in a few days. I will call you." "Chase, that was quite a story." "Obviously, you got back together." "Yes," he said, "But it took some doing." I said, "Tell me about it." Chase said he started a campaign to win her back, "What did you do to make that happen?" "I sent her gifts, lots of gifts, jewelry, a fur coat, all disguised and delivered by a messenger. "One time," Chase said, "I send her a beautiful ring hidden in a bouquet of flowers." "When the messenger returned to me, I asked him did she say anything?" "No," he said, "but she did throw the flowers away in the dumpster. I said, "You need to go back and tell her about the ring!"

"He did, and Amber had the messenger and several employees searching through the dumpster until they found the ring." I said to Chase, "You are such a romantic." Chase told me that eventually, Amber came back to him. "So," I said, you were really serious about Amber?"

Chase said, "I wanted to be, but I must tell you that for some time, I was living in two worlds, The Amber and I world, and the world where the memory of Kris was making me create so many hoops to put Amber through, I was surprised that she stayed around. "I would have never blamed her if she left me cold." I told Chase that it seemed to me that his relationship with Amber would fail as long as he could not put Kris away. What Chase told me next came as a bit of a surprise. Chase told me that Amber's boss told her to get rid of me that weekend, and he thought she was going to do it. "That Friday night, as Amber and I were having a very serious conversation," I felt she was going to tell me it was over between us." "Something just clicked in me, and I was afraid that I would lose her." "So, as I was sure it was coming into the conversation., I said to her, I think we should get married." "Whoa," I said, "had you thought that through?" Chase said, he didn't think so, he only knew he didn't want to let Amber go. "What did she say?" I asked him. "She said YES" "It was then," Chase said, "That for the first time I realized I was actually in love with this person." I had to admit, I was exhausted just from just listening. I said, "OK, let's pick this up at our next session. When Chase left, I thought about a new chapter in the Chase saga. I hoped it would be a good one, but to be honest, I wasn't sure.

CHAPTER TWENTY-TWO
THE REST OF THE STORY

I was concerned about Chase's decision to ask Amber to marry him. At that time, I felt he had not properly moved on from Kris, and I was just waiting for him to tell me that his marriage to Amber lasted for just a brief period. After all, from our discussion last time, I realized he and Amber had a very volatile relationship. I was going to make this my first area for discussion. "Chase," I said, "if you don't mind, could we explore in a little more detail your decision to ask Amber to marry you.?" He said, "I thought you might want to talk about that." "It just seemed to me you were not completely on board with your decision." "Am I reading this wrong?" "No," Chase said, "you have a valid point." "So, what was your motivation?" Chase told me that for a very long time, he believed he was punishing Amber for what Kris had done to him. I said, "You know that was not healthy or at the very least fair to Amber." "I know," he said, "But I just could not help myself. I was still hurt and angry at Kris, and I was bound and determined not to let any other woman do to me what Kris had done." "And you thought that by creating a volatile relationship with Amber, which would somehow make her love you more?" Chase said, "To tell you the truth, I didn't know." "I guess part of me was trying to drive her away, but she kept coming back." "Chase, maybe she loved you, and was just waiting for you to straighten out your act." "I guess," Chase said, "And in our relationship, I was truly sorry for what I had put her through." I asked Chase what was about Amber that made him think he could marry her. He told me he had reached the point in his life where he wanted a stable long-term relationship with someone who could give him a family. I told him we have never even discussed his desire for a family. "Doc," Chase said, "when I had the opportunity to spend time with Amber's family, I realized she was part of a very loving family who always stood by each other."

"I never had a family life like that. Mine was so dysfunctional." "I knew that if I married Amber, we could have a very successful family, and I really wanted that."

I told him I completely understood his motivation, and I was glad that Amber had come through his unreasonable gauntlet and was still willing to marry him. He told me he was glad too, but he would have completely understood if she told him to take a hike. "So," he said, "after all the craziness that comes with planning a wedding, we were finally married in July 1984. "We set up house, like married couples were supposed to do, and started our "together lifestyle." "Two years later my son was born, and I was the completely over the top father. In those days, I truly loved being married, and I truly loved Amber." I felt compelled to ask him, "what about Kris?" "Doc," he said, "you really have a knack for cutting right through to the heart of the matter." I said, "Chase, I am just trying to understand how stable a person you were at the time." "Let me explain it this way," he said. "What Kris and I had transcended time and place. She was my first love and the person who hurt me the most." "But I could never truly forget her, nor could I truly ever stop loving her." "Chase, "I said, "that was a lot of weight to carry around." "Yes," he said, "I was aware, but the heart has an amazing capacity to store love." "You see, the love I had with Kris was the love of my youth, the craziness, the carefree lifestyle, the live for today attitude." "The love I shared with Amber was the love I needed as ·an adult, complete with the responsibility that comes with a long-term relationship." I said, "Chase, you never fail to amaze me with your capacity to cope with your circumstances." Chase told me that five years later, with the birth of his daughter, he finally had the family he always wanted. "Paradise, right," I said. "Not quite," Chase responded with a stone-cold look on his face.

I did not discuss this with Chase, but I knew we were now getting into the area of his life that generated the most concern for his family. "Chase," I said, "Let's save the next part for our next session." Chase agreed and left with a silent demeanor.

After all this time with Chase, I still found him to be a very complicated person. He seemed at times to have it all together, and then, without a second thought, he is unable to function. I was most concerned however with his mental state. After years of tragic incidents, I was unsure as to how he was keeping it all together. There was a significant gap in time coming up that we needed to discuss.

As much as I now cared for Chase and the discussion I knew lay ahead, part of me dreaded the possibility of what would happen in our next session. Once again, I headed home, fixed a strong drink, and tried to find some peace.

CHAPTER TWENTY-THREE
THE REAL REAL

Chase came in this morning, and we shared a cup of tea. I didn't know if he drank tea anywhere outside my office, but here, he seemed to enjoy it. I said, "Chase, it is good to see you. I hope you are well." He said, "As well as expected." That statement might have been a harbinger of what was to come. I said, "how is the family?" "Good," he said, "My son is doing well in New York, and My daughter is really enjoying her tenth year of teaching." "Excellent," "I said. It is always a blessing when your children have succeeded." He nodded in agreement. "Well," where shall we go today?" I knew exactly where I wanted to take this discussion. After two years, I thought it was about time to get to the genuine issue in Chase's life. But I was going to let him carry me there, rather than push it.

"I want to jump ahead to a time when my world suddenly came to a brief stop, brief but ever so poignant." I told him I would welcome any part of his life that he wanted to discuss. He took a deep breath, looked around for a minute, and then began. "I was at a point in my life with Amber, which could only be described as pedestrian." "We had been married for about twenty-one years, and we were just motoring through life being the consummate parenting couple. "Was this a bad thing?" I asked. "No, just what it was." "Now please understand me, I had never considered another woman beyond Amber." "When I said, "I do," it was the same I do as I expressed with Kris." "I know, commitment." "Exactly," he said. "Well, I'll give you this. You are consistent." "So, did anything happen to shake that solid rock of yours?" This is where I believed the first sign of marital discord began. "Well, I was sitting at my desk at the high school I was teaching in, and I received a call from the office telling me I had a long-distance phone call, and could they put it through?" I wondered, "who do I know that would call me in the middle of the day at work, and where were they calling from?" I told the office to go ahead and put the call through. "There was a silence for a few seconds while the call connected, then I heard a voice say "Chase" "I nearly dropped the phone." "I knew immediately who it was. I could never forget the sound of that voice." "It was Kris." Although I suspected as much, I let Chase continue. "I said, Kris, it is good to hear your voice." "Really," she said, "I thought you would never want to hear my voice again." Chase said, "Come on Kris, it's been what, twenty-six years?" She said, "I did not think you were still counting, or that you even remembered me." "I did not respond to that statement." "So, tell me Kris, why are you calling me now, after all these years?" "I just needed to hear your voice." She said. "OK, you have heard it." "Wow," I said, "kind of cold, wasn't that?" Chase told me he was stunned and not doing well on the phone with Kris. "I just needed to contact you and tell you how profoundly sorry I was for ever leaving you." "It was a monumental mistake." Chase told me he didn't know what to say, but in his mind, he was thinking, "are you kidding me? It took you twenty-six years to come to that conclusion."

"I have been going through some major soul-searching, and I wanted to reach out to all those I have hurt in the past," "I instinctively asked. "How long is that list?" She said, "Not long, but the people on the list were important to me." Chase told me he was changing his demeanor and addressing Kris as a matter-of-fact event. "Ok Kris," he said. "It has been lovely speaking with you after all these years, but I have to get back to work." She said, "OK, but I just want you to know, I was dreading the next sentence that would come out of Chases' mouth. "That I still love you." And there it is, I thought. I needed to walk Chase down from whatever cloud he was on now.

I said, "Chase, first, how did you respond to her, and secondarily, how were you feeling after you heard Kris say those words?" He told me he was numb. He couldn't speak or do anything. Finally, he said to Kris," A little late, don't you think?" I knew Chase was just lashing out for Twenty-six years of silence. I chose not to address that statement. Kris said, "I don't blame you for being mad." Chase said, "I'm not mad, just numb." "I'm sorry Kris, It really is good to hear your voice." "And it is wonderful to hear yours." "Would you mind if I called you again?" Chase told me he was so torn. On the one hand, what was Kris trying to do, re-establish a relationship? And on the other, he was desperate to hear her voice." "What did you say to her?" "I told her she could call me again, if she needed to." She said, "Thank you, I will call again." "Is this a good number?" I said, "Yes, you can call me at this number." She said, "Thank you, Goodbye Chase. I said, "Goodbye, and hung up the phone.

"For several minutes, I couldn't move." "Then, despite where I was, I cried, and I didn't know how I was going to stop." "Then reality took over," He said. "I am so glad I told her to call me at this number." "Could you imagine if I gave her my cell number and Amber found out about it?" I said, "Would that be so bad?" "After all, you were married to her."

Chase said, "Doc, you know that all this time we have spent with each other, you had to know that Amber would never approve of me speaking with Kris.""Kris was her nemesis, the reason for all her struggles with me in the early days." "Amber felt she had won and was not about to let the enemy in again. "I said, "Sorry, I forgot for a minute that we were operating in the World of Chase." "So, did Kris in fact call you again?" "Yes, many times," Chase said. "And you never told Amber about the clandestine phone relationship you were having with your ex-wife." "No," said Chase. "Did she ever find out?" "Well, about six years after I reconnected with Kris, I told Amber that we were talking." "How did she take that?"

"She said she didn't care if I spoke with Kris." "Somehow, I had a hard time accepting her generous response." "But, then again," Chase said, "our marriage was not the Disney model of marriages." I told Chase that I understood that sometimes marriages morph into a shadow of their former selves." Chase said, "I never wanted that to happen, but truthfully, we let it get away. We both let our marriage get away." Even as Chase said those words to me, I could see the sorrow in his eyes. "Chase, thank you so much for sharing these last few hours. I know it was tough." "I think we should call it a day." Chase agreed, and I told him I would see him next week. As Chase left, I thought to myself once again, how does one person get through all that has happened to him, and still be able to function? I also thought, why did Chase wait so long before coming to see me? I wasn't exactly looking forward to our next session, but I knew I had to be there for it.

CHAPTER TWENTY-FOUR
THE PAST CATCHES UP WITH THE PRESENT

This morning, I decided to investigate a little further the choice Chase made to reconnect with Kris. I didn't feel comfortable with the way he described the event. The challenge I faced was to not push him over the edge, and then have to live with the fallout. This was going to be interesting.

"Good morning, Chase." "Good morning, Doc." "Care for some tea?" "Sure, I'd love a cup of your amazing tea." As we enjoyed our tea, I thought this would be a good time to tell Chase what we were going to cover in today's session. I only hoped he agree to speak more about it. "Chase, if you don't mind, I would like to go back to our last session and revisit your motivation for allowing Kris back into your life."

"Doc, I don't know what more I can add to make the story any more complete." "Chase, why don't we start and see if we can uncover any new information." Chase said, "Alright Doc, lead the way."

"I am interested in how you felt when you first heard Kris's voice after all that time. You said to her that it was good to hear her voice, "Were you just being cordial, or did you really mean what you said." "Before you answer, I would like to remind you of what you said the day Kris left you. Chase said, "Doc, you don't have to remind me of that day, I have played that day over and over in my mind for years." I said, "Chase, that is what I am talking about. Your grief over that day was nothing short of monumental." "You told me you didn't know if you could ever come back from that pain." "Doc, please don't do this, can't you just let it be and accept that I was over Kris and when she called, I was genuinely happy to hear her voice."

"Yes," I said, "I can accept what you are saying if in your heart, you truly believe that you could let Kris back into your life without some major problems." "I must continue Chase, even though I know this may be difficult to hear." "I believe that you thought that your marriage to Amber might be on the rocks, and you couldn't bear to be alone again. Kris would serve as the perfect fallback person." "It would be just like old times, except both of you were now older and wiser." "Chase, is what I am saying even remotely what you were considering?" After a few seconds, Chase responded, "Doc, I don't know if what you are saying was what I was thinking at the time." "I was just happy to hear Kris's voice." "Chase," I said, "I believe that you are being disingenuous with me. I have heard you say a number of times that you have never stopped loving Kris, and at the time of her phone call, she opened to door for a future relationship." "What did you think was going to happen?" "Did you think you could just hang up the phone and 'let it be' as you say, no harm, no foul.?" "Or were you thinking , as I believe, sure, please just walk back into my life." "Doc, please, we can't do this." "I'm not ready to discuss what I was feeling when Kris called." "As a matter of fact, I don't recall what I was thinking at the time, I only know that I heard her voice and I was happy." "That's right, happy, happier than I had been in a long time." Chase related to me that Kris had called him the next day to see if he was sure he wanted her to call him again. Chase, can you tell me about the substance of that phone call?" "Doc, please, can't you just leave this alone. I don't want to talk about Kris as it relates to her phone calls to me." "I think you understand me well enough to know when I am being serious." "All right," I said, "I will drop this for now, but you must understand what my job is in this relationship." "I am not supposed to stand by and watch you commit emotional suicide." I am supposed to care for your emotional needs and help you move forward without any damage to yourself or another in your party.?" Chase thanked Dr. Styles for not dragging around his spirit. But in his heart, he knew that what Chase was doing was going to cause a major problem for everyone who cared about him. The next session would be a strong emotional one.

CHAPTER TWENTY-FIVE
WHAT DO YOU SAY TO THE YEARS?

By now, it was clear that Chase and I had achieved a new level of understanding about his life. I thought little more could happen to this sensitive individual. It just goes to show you how wrong we can sometime be. I could tell that as soon as Chase came into the room, something was weighing heavily on his mind. "Are you alright Chase?" I asked. Chase looked at me and offered a faint smile. "Ok," I said, "Time for some tea." I got up to make the tea and I could see that Chase's eyes were bloodshot and he really seemed more fragile than usual. I said, "Chase, we really need to talk." He said, "I know, but it's so hard. With that, he put his head in his hands and seemed to sob. "I don't mean to pry, but it is my job. Why don't you try telling me why you are so upset?" He said he had been on the phone with Kris almost all night. I said, "So, you really have been engaging her in conversation on a regular basis." "Yes" he said. "I know it's not healthy, but I just can't stop." "There is something about Kris that haunts me every day" "I can't adequately describe how, but I need to hear her voice constantly." This was becoming a psychosis, and I needed to get more information before I could proceed." "What is it about her voice that is so enticing to the point of almost becoming an addiction?" "I am not sure," he said, "But it happened the very first time we spoke almost fifty years ago."

I swear," he said, it is hypnotic, and always comforts me no matter what emotional state I am in." "Well," I said, "It sounds like you have your hands full here." "How do you see this playing out?" "I don't know, and that's what's killing me." "Tell me this, has she asked to see you?" "Not yet, but she said she was coming to Florida in a couple of months." Now, I understood the emotional tug-of-war Chase was going through." "Were you planning to see her?" "God, I didn't know." "Part of me wanted to badly, but another part of me knew that this would be a terrible idea." "Doc, I'm in awful shape!" "I can't eat. I don't sleep more than a couple hours a night. Everything I used to take for normal now seems to be upside down." "I don't know if I am going to make it." I said, "Chase, let's step back from this for a moment." "Take a deep breath and let's try to focus on a solution," "He said, "Doc, I don't think there is a solution." "What solution could there possibly be, where I come out of it whole again?" "Chase," I said, "I have always considered myself to be an optimist, and as such, determined to find the win-win in the most difficult of situations." "Well, good luck." He said. "Have you considered talking to Amber about all of this?"

"oh doc, oh doc, oh doc, why don't you just ask me to go and stab her repeatedly." "Chase," I said, "I'm pretty sure it's not that bad." "no Doc, take my word for it, it is this bad."

I felt for a moment that Chase was losing touch with reality. I knew if I could not psychologically talk him down, he might go so far out there, he couldn't return. "Chase, would you like me to talk to Kris?" "I'm not sure what good that would do." Well, does she know the effect she is having on you?" "Yes. I have told her." "And what was her response?" "She was sorry that she could not be with me," "Was that It?" "No," Chase said, "She also told me if it was going to be a problem, then she would stop talking to me." "Wow." I said. "There are certainly few positive choices there." Chase just looked up at me.

"Chase," Can we talk about anything else concerning your life that doesn't have Kris in it?" I had hoped he understood my heart. It wasn't that I didn't know how important Kris was to him. It was just too much drama to deal with at this moment, with very little payoff. "I believe," Chase said, "That there are a few more things to discuss." "I am more than willing to hear what you have to say" "I want you to understand what happened to Amber and me over time." Chase said. "I have already established the notion of shared blame for our circumstances." "You know what," he said, "blame is not the right word." "There is no blame in this story, and to prescribe blame would do a great disservice to Amber and me." "The truth is, as I have already mentioned, rested with Amber's decisions and my decisions."

"We collectively lost the essence of our marriage." "Whether it was due to too much work, or not enough family time." "Or a purposeful desire to have our own independence." "We both gave up on each other." "We lost confidence in each other." "And, most importantly, we forgot how to depend on each other." I know that these are the elements of disaster."

"I will try to express our situation in this manner," "At some point, when was not important, Amber loved me but was not in love with me." "I hope you can detect the subtle difference." "I, on the other hand, remained in love with Amber for a longer period." "But, when couples reach this point, their marriage is just a shadow of its former self, and the parties involved morph their relationship into a living, breathing, functioning lie." "The problem is that neither party will let go, and so they go about their business, taking great pains not to upset the apple cart." "For Amber, I believe she stayed in this relationship because there is no cost to her. There is no longer any investment in quite frankly…me" "She was free to come and go as she pleased with no responsibility to…me." "Chase, I am sorry once again." "God, I am so tired of apologizing for what the world has done to you and your relationships." "Doc, he said, "It's OK, it's part of the game." Then I asked Chase, what keeps you in this relationship?" He said, "That's easy…Commitment." "I almost cried."

CHAPTER TWENTY-SIX
UNINTENDED CONSEQUENCES

I must admit that my last session with Chase was more eye- opening than any other before it. He spoke so eloquently about the ending of a marriage, while still being married. My professional training would suggest that this kind of dialogue is dangerous on several fronts. It's delusional. And yet, they are still together. My colleagues would suggest that this kind of behavior can't possibly last. And yet, Chase and Amber recently had their 40th wedding anniversary. My own relationship with Chase has revealed to me that there are so many forces at work in his life. It is a wonder how he can still function in any capacity.

When Chase came in this morning, I expressed to him my feelings about our last encounter. I said to him, "Chase, do you think you could come up with a rational discussion concerning the events that have transpired in your life?" Chase thought about it for a minute, and then a little longer. It seemed like his brain was going a mile a minute. Finally he said. "Doc, this may sound very simplistic, but the reason for what has transpired (your words), during the course of my life can be attributed to the theory of Unintended Consequences."

I handed him my writing portfolio, the one I used to take notes during sessions, and said. "Wow, you should just take over now. I totally applaud your response." Chase laughed, but he knew that was I being sincere. "Look Doc," he said, I have chosen not to dwell on the events that have shaped my life for fear of what I might do." I said, "Chase, as a professional therapist, those words might get you in trouble." Chase said, "I want you to understand that I am in control of my destiny." "No matter what happens to me, I decide how to manage it."

Those words from Chase seemed troubling to because of their finiteness. "Even my relationship with Kris is of my own doing." "Can you elaborate on that a bit?" Sure," he said, "About fifteen years ago, I could have left Amber and been with Kris." "Kris had come to Florida to settle some real estate business. Her sister and her sister's family came as well. I asked Amber if she minded if I went to meet them for dinner." Amber to me. She did not care if I went or not." "Now, you know that a wife's statement like that is code for "you better not go!" "However, I was playing dumb, because I really wanted to see Kris." "So I went and had a great time." "But that was not all."

"Once I saw Kris again, all my emotions for her, and I mean the ones that took place before the divorce, came rushing back to me. I couldn't stand to be any more than a foot away from her." "I know her sister saw it right away."

"Chase," I said, "didn't you think this was a dangerous behavior to engage in?" "Of course, but I didn't care." "I wanted Kris to know that I still had a great deal of love for her."She knew, and I honestly believed that we could be together again." "That night, I went home and told Amber that I didn't know if I wanted to continue to be married to her." "She just looked up and left the bedroom." "The next few weeks were hell."

"I had a decision to make and Amber was not going to have any influence on my decision." "I knew this because she refused to discuss the matter with me at all." "Chase," I said, "I did not know how you managed to stay off some therapist's couch." "How did you resolve this situation?" "I spoke with Kris several times over the next few weeks and she was kind, but also told me that the decision had to be mine and mine alone." "After many hours of contemplation, and very little sleep, I decided not to leave Amber." "How did Kris take the news?"

"Well, that was a moment in history that I am not very proud of." Chase paused, "I let Kris know in a letter that I sent to her." "Along with the letter, was the broken cell phone that I used to communicate with her." "I was such a coward!" "I told her that she could not communicate with me anymore." "That the pain would be too great." When I got home, I told Amber about my decision not to leave her." "She said ok, in a very business-like manner." "I knew I was going to pay a high price for my foolishness, and I did." "Chase," I said, "I am stunned, stunned but not surprised." I told him the continuous love he had for Kris was bound to cause him major problems. "So," he said, "During that period of time in my life, I had no communication with Kris and little to no communication with Amber. As the session came to a close, I said to Chase, "So, do you still want to cling to your theory of Unintended Consequences?" Chase smiled, but I knew I hurt him. That was a cruel thing to say. I swear, by this time, I needed my own therapist.

CHAPTER TWENTY-SEVEN
I CAN'T FIND THE WORDS

It was a little more than two years into my relationship with Chase, when I thought, maybe he needs a new therapist. I had become so attached to him as a patient, and also as a friend. I knew the rules, never get personally involved with your patients. But I could not help myself, at times, I felt as if I were the only friend that Chase had. What we have been through during our sessions over the last two years was truly remarkable. I cared deeply for Chase but I was beginning to feel as if there was nothing left for me to offer. I was not sure if this was the right decision, but I did believe I should offer it to Chase.

When Chase came in today, we shared a cup of tea as usual. As we sat down, I said to him, "Chase, if you don't mind, I would like to discuss something with you." He said that would be fine. "We have been together for quite some time now, and I am feeling as if we are in a Psychological rut." "Doc," Chase said, "Are you trying to get rid of me?" I said, "Chase I do not want to get rid of you, as you put it, I want to discuss the possibility that there might be another therapist who could be of more help to you." " In what way?" he asked. "To be honest with you, I am in some regard feeling too close to you and your situation." "In other words, I am afraid I might give you support that might not be in keeping with the best clinical practice protocol because of emotional attachment to you." Chase responded, "Doc, I can't tell you how much I appreciate that you are willing to get down in the trenches with me and be a real person, not just a walking, talking protocol." I told Chase that

I appreciated his sentiment, but he should understand that I at times have felt that I have violated my own official therapist position, by not being able to see the big picture as an objective observer.

I could see that Chase was becoming uncomfortable with this discussion. He was displaying classic symptoms of withdrawal and a lack of trust concerning my position. Chase, then almost sheepishly said, "Doc, I don't need an objective observer, I need someone who is as souled out to my needs even if it means getting into my skin with me," "Do you think I could have come here all this time, week after week and bared my soul to just an observer." "I need to know that you care as much about me and my problems as I have come to care about and trust that you always have my best interests at heart. Mark the word heart." I knew that for the first time with Chase, he was completely baring his heart and soul and offering me a place there. I felt like a ton of bricks had just fallen on me, and I was so involved with what I thought and what I needed, that I forgot about what Chase needed. I tried to make amends. "Chase," I said, "I am sorry that I let you down. It was never my intention. I will always want what is best for you without worrying about what process it takes to get there. I hope you will forgive me and allow us to continue." Chase very quietly got up and headed for the door. "Doc," he said, "I think we need a break." With that he walked out. I have never felt a sense of loss like I did that day. I wondered if Chase would be back. If we could continue as we have in the past. I wondered if I had lost his trust. I knew we had more to cover in his therapeutic journey. I was worried that we might not be able to move past my stupidity. And, if he returned, would we have the same relationship, or would I have to rebuild that relationship all over again? For the first time in a long time, I had only questions and no answers. No professional jargon, no clinical suggestions. I felt more like a patient than a therapist, and I was not happy with myself. I could only hope that Chase would call in and arrange for a new appointment. I promised myself, if he did, that I would never do anything again that might drive him away. But what would I say to him? What would be the necessary conversation that could allow us to essentially begin again. I thought, at this moment in time, I can't find the words.

I knew that it was going to take more than a strong drink to get over this day. I had my secretary cancel the rest of my appointments for this day, and I left the office.

CHAPTER TWENTY-EIGHT
WHICH PART OF I'M SORRY...

It had been thirty days since Chase walked out of my office and essentially out of my life. I was a bit distraught to say the least. How could I have been so insensitive to this fragile human being to forget about his needs, in favor of mine. I was truly lost in a turmoil of my own making. I tried two or three times to pick up the phone and call Chase, but I hesitated. If he didn't want to speak to me, the phone call was just another insult.

If he wanted something from me, could I make sure that could supply it? I decided to wait another week to see if anything would happen. A couple of days later, the phone rang and it was Chase. I didn't even get the chance to say hello. "Doc, this is Chase, I need to see you right away!" I said, hello Chase, when do you want to come in?" "How about Now!" Chased said. I could sense a tremendous amount of emotion in Chase's voice. "Chase, I said, It is 8:30 in the evening." "I'll be there in thirty minutes." He didn't wait for confirmation, he just hung up the phone. I couldn't believe it, but I knew I had to see him. If for no other reason than to find out what this was all about.

True to his word, Chase showed up a half hour later. He knocked on my door, and I opened it to see the face of my friend who was clearly distraught. "Chase, please come in." Let me put on some tea for us." "Not right now," Chase said. He then went right to my couch and sat down. I followed him and asked," "Chase please tell me how I can help you, you are clearly in pain," It almost seemed as if he could not speak.

He tried a couple of times and nothing came out. I said, "Chase, before you hyperventilate, please calm down and give yourself time to process your thoughts. I'm not going anywhere; We can have all night." Chase seemed to calm down a bit and his breathing slowly returned to normal. "All right Chase, when you are ready, I am here listening." Chase told me what had been going on. It seems that he and Amber had been fighting for about a week over what he considered to be nonsense. "Chase, what kind of nonsense are you referring to?" "Doc, stupid things that couples fight over all the time. But this week, I was not in the mood for Amber's rantings." " I told her she needed to stop and consider the kind of hurt she was inflicting on me, and I was not going to accept it." "She stormed out of the room, only to come back moments later to announce, "You want out of this marriage, I give you permission. You can leave at any time." I told Chase once again how sorry I was for his circumstance. He said, "Doc, I was shocked over Amber's callous statement." "How did you respond to her?" "I didn't, and I stared at her for a few seconds and then I left the room." "Amber followed me and continued, "Why don't you just admit it, you don't want to be married to me anymore." "Just admit the defeat!" "You tried you best, but your best just wasn't good enough." "I hereby free you from you precious "Commitment!!" Chase said, "Those words burned through me like a sharp knife." Then Amber said, "Oh yeah, when you finally decide to go, I give you permission to go to your first and only true love, Kris!" "I won't stop you!" I did not know what to do. I was blind with anger and not in control of any part of me. "I got in my car, drove down the road and pulled over."

"I was crying so hard; I couldn't see the road." I knew Chase was building up to something much more dramatic than his fight with Amber. "Chase, tell me what you did next." "I called Kris" he said. I knew he would do this; he had no love left with Amber. He had no comfort from anybody. All he had left was his dammed commitment! "What did you say to Kris?" "I told her the whole story, including why I was not able to leave up to this point." "Kris," I said. "Up to now, you have assumed that I was still with Amber because of my belief in commitments" Kris said, "There was nothing I was surer of in my life." Then Chase said, "I am so sorry to disappoint you, but commitment was only a small part of the story." "The reason I was not able to leave Amber was because, If I left, I would be alone." "Yes," Kris said, "I'm listening." "Then, I would come to you, and I have told you many times that if I left Amber, which is exactly what I would do." Kris said, "I remember you saying those exact words." "My greatest fear, and the real reason that I never left Amber, was because, If I did, you would not be there for me." "And frankly, I could not manage that ." "Doc, then Kris said words I never thought I'd hear. "Kris said, Chase, You must do what is right for you, without regard to what anyone else might think." "You don't owe anything to anybody, and whatever it takes to make you whole, is what you should pursue." "Even if it is you that I need?" Chase said to her. "Chase, "she said, "I have lived alone for a very long time, and I quite frankly I have gotten used to that kind of lifestyle." I thought to myself, Oh my God, she's writing him off!" "I don't have the right to tell you what to do." I could just see Chases' heart being crushed as he is telling me this story. Chase said to her, "The right! The right!, Who is talking about rights!, I am talking about love!!!" Kris said, "Chase, I understand your position, I just don't want to give any kind of false hope," "Kris!" Chase said, I am talking about us!" Chase told me there was silence on Kris's side of the phone. After a few minutes Kris said, "Chase, let's not worry about this right now," "Consider your options and call me when you have a plan." Chase was now way around the bend. The true love of his life had just reduced him to less than nothing. "Doc," he said, "The last statement she made was one you would say to an architect who was adding a room on to your house." Now, I knew that Chase's worst nightmare had finally come true. He had lost Amber and he was about to lose Kris. I knew he would need intense care for the foreseeable future." "I said Chase, please don't call this the end of you and Kris."

"Give her a few days to process what you have told her. Then, call her and discuss it further." "In the next few days, please stay close to me. Even if you need to see me every day, I am here for you." Chase looked at me for a few minutes with the most pain-driven eyes I had ever seen. "Chase, is there anyone I could call for you?" Chase let out a quiet but poignant laugh." "Who could you possibly call that would understand what I am going through more than you." I said, "I thank you for the confidence, but I was speaking about someone in your family." "Doc," he said, "As far as I am concerned, I have no family," "and right now, I have no future." I told Chase to consider not talking for a number of days, I would get back to him with a new schedule. He said, "Doc, thank you for always being in my corner, you have no idea what your friendship and support have meant to me these past few years."

"Chase, "I said, "I love you like a brother. Now let me at least find you a hotel you can stay in for the next few days, in order to get your head straight." Chase said, "Thank you, I love you too." As Chase was lying on my couch, he fell asleep. Who could blame him? He had been through one of the worst sessions I had ever seen. I wished with all my heart, that I could block out what I had seen and heard, But that would not be fair to Chase. I got on my phone and booked Chase a room and called for an Uber to take him there. But I told the uber driver to wait a couple of hours. I knew Chase was exhausted and needed to recharge. I will see him in a few days. I saw Chase off and asked him to please relax and not talk to anybody until I saw him again. He agreed and gave me a quiet smile. I knew that Chase was a broken human being and needed my help. I only hoped that I could find a way to help him establish a new peaceful covenant with life. I would try my very best to bring him home.

CHAPTER TWENTY-NINE
WHAT DO WE DO WITH THE REST OF OUR LIVES

The next day, I remembered to check on Chase. He was exhausted but glad to be in a safe place. I told him that I would be sending him some food and drink and please do not venture out unless it was absolutely necessary. He agreed and thanked me again for being a good friend. As he hung up the phone, I said to myself, "Some good friend. I drove him away, and just when he needed me the most, I wasn't there. He was left to suffer on his own, and I did nothing to help him." I need to write a brand-new definition for "good friend." The next day, I went to the hotel to see Chase. He was still exhausted but making progress. I said, "Chase, do you need anything at all?" He told me he was ok, and felt he was getting better each day. I said I was glad to hear it, and for him to let me know when he was ready to resume our sessions. He said, "Doc, I'm not sure I want to come back to our old ways of doing our sessions." "What do you mean?" I said. "Well, I think we need a "new normal" for me to use as a reference point." "Certainly, my old existence has been shot to hell and I definitely don't want to go back to that." I told him that I completely understood his reasoning, and if he would give me a few days, I would try my hardest to produce a plan that we could both utilize. He said thank you and he would look forward to meeting with me again. After I left, I couldn't help but think that Chase had already constructed an alternative life for himself. That, to me was scary as hell. I knew the research and that when people "check out" from their current existence, the new normal they construct is rarely successful. As a matter of fact, in many cases, it leads to a very permanent ending. I made the conscious decision to check in with Chase at least twice a day.

About a month later, Chase called to say that he wanted to meet in my office the next Monday. I told him I would clear my schedule and that he was completely welcome to come in at any time during that day. "By the way," I said, "How is your new normal treating you?" "Actually, quite well." I said, "I am glad to hear it." "I will be waiting for you with tea," Chase laughed, "you are such a tease, see you on Monday."

Monday came and so did Chase, around 1 o'clock in the afternoon. I greeted him as warmly as I could and asked him to sit wherever he would be most comfortable. He thanked me and graciously received his tea. "Wow, I remember this tea, thank you for being so considerate." I smiled and sat down across from him. "First of all, Chase," I said, "I am so grateful to see you in this office once again." "It and I have missed you." Chase said, "Thank you Dr. Styles," I was taken by surprise, Chase rarely referred to me by my full professional name before." "Maybe, this was part of his new normal, and I wasn't beyond accepting a complement, It was refreshing."

"Chase, if you don't mind, could you explain your expectations for our new relationship. He said, "Well you know my previous relationships are all but gone now and I need to find a new home for my feelings." "I completely understand where you are coming from, and I am ready and willing to assist you in any way that I can. "I said "Thank you ," he said. "OK, I'm all ears, explain the next step in the process." Chase took a deep breath and swallowed the last of his tea. "Well for starters, I think out doctor-patient relationship should morph into a James and Chase partnership." "A partnership, I asked?" "Yes," "OK, how would this partnership work?" "You and I would be friends with no judgement ever." "We would spend time in this office, and sometimes outside this office exploring the wonderful world of…. Well, everything." "I am intrigued." I said. "What would be the purpose of such a venture?" I asked. "The purpose, he said, would be to share experiences and share feelings." "You remember feelings, don't you?" I told him I absolutely remember feelings." Well, feelings need to be our guiding force if we are to be successful." "I can appreciate your point" I said, "But would we have a mission, or a purpose from which to catalogue these feelings?" "Do we need some higher authority dictating what our actions should be. After all, no higher authority did anything for my previous relationships. The ones I gave my whole for without regard for myself." "Chase," I said, "you don't have to do this." "It's not healthy and it won't help your situation." "James," he said," Please, let me finish." I knew that Chase has constructed a new normal that was designed to be without people. No one could ever get to him again, to hurt him or desert him. In his new world, he would never fail. Never be lonely because he was protecting himself from all adversaries. I had seen something like this before, but never to this degree. He had absolutely no relationships, except with me if I agreed to the terms of the new Chase world view. I knew now that Chase was operating in a totally new universe, devoid of any real feelings, because feelings only work when applied to others in our lives, so that they can share and appreciate us. Chase needed no such appreciation. As a matter of fact, he would shun any and all relationships that required feelings as motivation.

I was beside myself thinking how did he construct this? People take years to remove themselves from their society. Chase did it in a matter of weeks. I had to ask him, "Chase, what makes you think you'd be happy in your new reality?" Chase responded, "It's a piece of cake, there is no one to stop me from having a good time. Not only are there great experiences to explore, but also no possibility of failure. The reason you need a new reality is because in the new Chase world, no one ever needs your services, "I'm telling you James, it's the perfect world."

After hearing all about Chases' new world reality, I was absolutely floored. The level of hurt from both Amber and Kris completely removed his reality function. He was in essence, a ghost of his former self, and I knew he could not sustain this behavior for very long. "Chase," I said, are you interested in seeing any of your family?" "I'm sure they would love to hear about how you are doing." Chase told me that he would rather stay anonymous for the time being.

"If all goes well, I might invite them into my world out of courtesy." "But for now, You are the only one I want to share in my good fortune." I knew that Chase was going down a very dark road, and he might not be able to come back from the damage. I had to find a way to convince him that this was going in the wrong direction. I didn't know for sure how much time I had before Chase was no longer a viable patient. "All right Chase," I said, "let's leave your world alone for the time being. We can always come back any time we want, correct? "Absolutely, "he said. "Great," I said. "I am going to send you the contact information for a few locations that will make sure that you have all your needs met. Would you do me a favor and visit some of them and see in what ways

129

they might help you." Chase told me he didn't see the need for these associations, but he would comply with my directions. I told chase that we would meet again in a couple of weeks. He said that he would be traveling, but he would be in town on the dates he would be needed. I told him thanks.

As he left my office, I knew he would have a hard time fitting in with the world of individuals who weren't dedicated to the Chase Roman Experience. I had to find a way to make him see the damage he had experienced had skewed his perspective of the world and he needed help to bring him home. I promised myself to help him find himself again.

CHAPTER THIRTY
IF I FORGET TO TELL YOU

I spent the next couple of weeks studying literature concerning what I considered to be Chases' primary condition, which contained living in an alternative universe. I also spoke to a number of colleagues about the subject. This included my friend Dr. Standford. "Mike," I said," Have you ever heard of this kind of condition to the extent of what I am revealing to you now?" Dr. Standford thought for a minute, "No, not really." I agreed and told him about how far Chase had moved away from reality central. Dr. Stanford said to me, "From what you are telling me James, It is clear that your patient has a very serious condition." "I hear your words and I am in total agreement. The problem, is how to move Chase away for his new reality without him crashing and burning." Mike said that he wished me well and would be available if I need to speak further. He also said that if I wanted him to get involved on a deeper level, including meeting with Chase, he would. He added, "Please understand, a meeting with your patient would involve many sessions," I agreed and said, "It took him years to develop this condition." "I'm sure it would take a significant amount of time to unpack it all and restore Chase, if possible, to a more normal status." Mike agreed and said he felt the operative word in my last sentence was "If." I knew exactly what he was talking about. You see, I genuinely felt that I could help Chase, but I was under no illusion that I could bring him back one hundred percent to Chase who first walked into my office so long ago. I must say that I too was hurting inside because I was unable to see the inevitability of where Chase would wind up and my inability to move him away from danger. It was almost like watching a terrible car accident that you didn't want to see, but one in which you were unable to turn away from. But I also knew that Chase needed my help more now than in any time during our relationship together. I must admit, I was afraid that I might not be able to help him, and that would leave me questioning my abilities that I had taken so long to develop. I knew that I was a good therapist but was I good enough for Chase. I guess only time would tell.

Sometime later, in the mail that my secretary brought into my office, was a letter from Chase. I opened it with great anticipation. It had been a couple of months since Chase left on his "world tour," and I was very curious to hear how it was going. As I opened the letter, a small flash drive fell out onto my desk. In the letter, were the words, " Doc, I miss you, please open this." I thought cool. Let's see what my friend has sent to me. As the flash drive was loading onto my computer, my anticipation was growing. What opened up was a video. This seems interesting. The video began this way. Chase was sitting at a desk in what looked like an upscale hotel or resort. He was wearing comfortable tropical attire, and I thought, good he is finally relaxing. "Hi Doc." He began, I hope this video finds you in good health and in good spirits. "I am doing as well as can be expected." "But enough about me."

"Doc, I wanted to take this time to thank you for everything you have done for me. Including the times you tried to tell me the truth, and I was too stubborn to listen.

I knew you always had my best interests at heart, and would never consciously hurt me, or lead me in a direction that would be unprofitable to me." You have been a great therapist, and I am proud to say an even better friend." Spending the past few months traveling has shown me that there is a world full of possibilities, if one is willing to seek them out." I thought, this is the Chase I wanted to hear from. " I am grateful to have had the chance to see for myself what you had been trying to tell me during our precious time together." "I know that my life had been so tightly wrapped around all the negative things that happened to me, which forced me to relate to only a few individuals." "Then when those individuals let me down, I no longer had a frame of reference for which to see life." "And life is so precious." "Please Doc, don't waste yours on anything that doesn't make you happy." "I want you to be happy," "So happy that you never have time for even a single negative thought to enter your mind, and lord knows I provided enough of those for you." That brought a smile to my face as I thought, "Yes, you certainly did, but I wouldn't have missed it for the world." 'I want you to know, that I don't blame Kris for not accepting me." 'After all, she had constructed a life all her own, and it was working for her. I had no right to change that, no matter how strongly I loved her."

I felt sad that Chase had never achieved what he might have if he and Kris were allowed to be together, without any outside influence. "I also can't blame Amber for the feelings she had towards me at the end. She did not deserve the kind of anguish I put her through, especially after all she went through to have a relationship with me." "I am profoundly sorry for the way I treated the only women who ever really loved me." I thought, "Chase, don't beat yourself up too badly, your intentions were always honorable, you just got lost along the way. "I am the one who is profoundly sorry that I was not able to provide the kind of support you ultimately needed."

Chase continued, "In the final analysis, this journey has taught me that life can be reduced to just about the choices we make. They are neither good nor bad, until we have had time to play them out." I wanted to tell him how proud I was of his ability to come out of a very dark place into the light of day. I thought, "If I get the chance, I will make copies of this flash drive and send them to Kris and Amber." I was not sure if that act was on Chase's mind as something to do. I couldn't find out or even suggest it to him until I saw him again, and who knew how long that would be. I thought they needed closure, and a knowledge of how far Chase had come emotionally. I wrote it down on my pad of things to do. Then Chase said, "Doc, I didn't mean to take up this much of your time, I just wanted to update you and tell you how much I have appreciated your friendship over the years." " I am feeling much better these days as I now know what lies ahead for me." "The future, as you have said, is always full of possibilities." "All we have to do is choose and hang on." "Doc, if I forget to tell you," he paused for a few seconds, "I love you. "Goodbye Doc."

As the video ended, I thought, "What an uplifting message." "Chase has finally reached what appears to be a significant level of peace in his life." "Something he was so hard pressed to do all those years." I wondered how long it would be before I had the chance to see him again and tell him in person how proud of him, I was."

I knew that when the time was right, he'd just come into the office, grab a cup of tea, and sit down like always. I could hardly wait for that moment. Chase's video absolutely made my day. I was sure I was going to share it with Dr. Stanford. After all, he had a part to play in Chases' life, and I felt he deserved to know how far Chase has come in his journey of life tour. I put his name on the list of people I wanted to see the video.

In the next few days, I sent the video to Kris and Amber. I included a note that read, "I thought you should see this video, in the hope that it would bring some peace to your heart." "You may feel free to contact me, if you would like to discuss the content of this video in greater detail."

Yours with great respect,
Dr. James Styles

I included my contact information, and actually thought, "I would love to meet these two women, not at the same time of course, but to get a glimpse of what Chase saw in them so long ago." I was pretty certain neither of them would contact me, but just in case, I wanted to offer them the opportunity. It was now getting near the end of the day, and I wanted to make myself a cup of tea before heading home. As I poured the water for the tea, so many images of Chase started flashing over and over in my mind. Images of him grabbing his cup and then sitting down for our latest session. Making fun of our necessary "tea preamble." I now know just how precious was the time that I spent with Chase in this office and how much of my life was occupied by him. I couldn't wait to see him again. I hoped he wouldn't make me wait too long.

After a while, I received a note from Kris, thanking me for the video, and for the time I spent with Chase. I never received a note from Amber. Well, I thought, I'm at least glad that one of them got the video and was kind enough to reach out to me. Perhaps, after a while, Kris would want to talk about her time with Chase. Just perhaps. Another week went by and It was just sort of life getting back to normal, whatever normal is supposed to be. Chase was really my only client now and I just spent the rest of my time consulting on cases for other colleagues.

My secretary came in and said, "I have a person on the phone named Kris, she wants to speak with you. "OK," I said, "Please put her through." "Wow," I thought, this could be very cool. As I picked up my end of the phone, I heard, "Dr. Styles, this is Kris." "Kris, It so lovely to speak with you at this time." "I feel as if I know you already." "What can I do for you?" A pause came over the line… "Dr. Styles, I need to tell you that last night, Chase took his own life…He left a note that said only "I'm sorry," Along with my phone number." "The police contacted me and asked if I could come down and identify the body." "I am on my way over there now." "I just thought you would want to know." And then I could hear the tears in her voice, "Goodbye Dr. Styles." And then nothing. I put the phone down, and reached for the letter from Chase that was still on my desk. The one that said, "I miss you" and I cried.

Postscript:

After the funeral, I had a chance to finally meet and talk with Kris and Amber. I found them very cordial and I told them how very sorry I was for their individual losses. Kris asked if I saw Chase around the time he decided to take his own life. I told her I saw Chase a couple of months before he died. "Oh" she said, "Did you have any idea that this was a possibility for him?" I told her I did not think he would go this far, since, during our whole time together, we never once had a conversation about this topic. And I told her that when I received the video, the same one I sent to her and Amber, Chase seemed rational and quite positive about his circumstances. She thanked me and said goodbye. I said, "Kris, you know if you ever want to talk about Chase, in any regard, I would be here for you." She said, "Thank you, but Chase and I had a love that transcended any normal relationship, and I just don't think you could ever understand." I knew she was wrong, but I let it go. Amber never engaged me in any further conversation other than our initial five minute one. I wondered if she blamed me for any part of what happened to Chase. But that was probably a whole nother' story, and I did not want to discuss it with her. I let it go, and I let Kris and Amber go. In the days and weeks that followed, I reviewed my notes for the entire period Chase was with me. I was looking for anything that could explain his behavior. I never did find any concrete evidence of what some would call, "A death wish." Sure, I did find examples of what we in the industry would call depression. I found that day one. But I always believed that through therapy, Chase could find himself whole again, and be able to live a productive life. Last week, Dr. Mike Stanford called and he told me he had read about Chase and the funeral. He asked if I was all right and did I need any help. "Mike," I said, "Thanks for the offer. Don't therapists always need help." It's an occupational hazard." He laughed and said, "Fair enough." "How about dinner next week?" I said, "Love to, I will call you for a time and place." After I hung up, I thought "Mike is a good friend and I immediately heard Chase's voice in my head, "Please Doc, don't waste your time on anything that doesn't make you happy." I wrote in my appointment book, dinner with Mike Stanford, a definite. I know now that what was important in my relationship with Chase was what we gained from each other. I will never forget the time I spent with him. He changed my life forever, and I hoped and prayed that in some small way, I had a positive impact on him. I now know that my friend Chase will always be with me, and… I wouldn't have it any other way.

I spent a few sleepless nights thinking about Chase and why I could not see what was going to happen, or why I could not reach him in the end. I kept thinking I was going to retire and could have done without this pain. But then I would have missed the most incredible exchange of my life. I came to the conclusion that although I told Chase that our sessions would remain private, I felt an overwhelming compulsion to share the lessons I had learned while working with Chase. I genuinely felt that much of what we had discovered together about the human condition could be beneficial to the others who were suffering in silence. I decided for the first time in my life to violate my own policy and find a way to tell the story of Chase Roman. If you are reading this, "Please, don't waste your time on anything that doesn't make you happy.

Dr. James Styles

AUTHOR BIO

Dr. Dennis Wechter has been an educator for over thirty years. He has earned five college degrees, including a Doctorate in Education. As an author, he has written three books, and numerous musical compositions. His passion has always been for music and writing. "I am at my best, when I am creating." He is married and has two children. This book is his first work of fiction. He is currently at work on a screenplay based on his second book.